DAISY MADIGAN'S PARADISE

Praxos Academy

SG TURNER

Daisy Madigan's Paradise
A Praxos Academy novella
SG Turner

Published by Chill Out Press
Copyright SG Turner 2012

❊   I   ❦

Sitting at the front of the class before her classmates arrived, Daisy Madigan opened her art coursework folder and pulled out a drawing she'd done at the weekend. Staring at it, she remembered how the lion had looked so peaceful, sleeping on the plinth in the park.

As the other kids started to enter the room noisily, she wished she could go back there and sit beneath it. It was her favourite statue at Abney Park. Nobody mocked her while she was there. Nobody cared that she had red curly hair. And freckles.

Once everyone had settled down, the usual routine began. Some of the kids started to throw things at her. Just little things so the teacher wouldn't notice. Rolled up pieces of paper, paper clips, broken erasers. Over the years she'd learned to ignore them. She just sat and listened to what the teacher had to say about the creative process of working with charcoal.

But before Mr Parker had even finished his sentence, the door opened and in walked a woman in her late fifties with huge eyes and a short, sleek black bob. For some reason, she reminded Daisy of those little Lego people she'd played with as a child. Not that you could play with Mrs Goodyear. She was the Headmistress.

Daisy watched as the middle-aged woman seemed to avoid all eye contact with the pupils, instead, making a beeline for Mr Parker. She didn't look happy. A certain sadness tinged her eyes.

Someone sniggered behind her and this time, a pencil whistled by Daisy's ear, landing on her desk before it rolled noisily on to the floor. It almost echoed in the room as everyone sat waiting quietly, wondering what was going on.

'Daisy?' asked Mrs Goodyear.

Surprised at hearing her name, Daisy looked up to see both teachers looking at her sadly.

'Daisy, please gather your belongings together and come with me.'

Without a word, she did as she was told. The other kids sniggered and made lame jokes quietly behind her back.

'Silence!' shouted Mr Parker as he banged his fists noisily on the desk in front of him, making poor little Amy Green nearly pee her pants.

Mr Parker never shouted, not at anyone.

All the kids looked up in shock, even the big bullies who resided at the very back of the classroom. 'Leave the poor girl alone,' he said as Daisy gently closed the door behind her.

She glanced through the window and smiled at him gratefully before turning her attention back to Mrs Goodyear.

'Please come with me, Daisy.'

The long walk down the corridor was like walking on death row. Had she done something wrong? They passed class upon class until they eventually arrived at the headmistress's office. It was the first time she'd ever found herself there. Glancing around, she wasn't particularly impressed by what she saw. It was a small, sparse room with nothing but several filing cabinets, a desk and a few chairs. The walls were painted stark white. Daisy shivered.

'Please sit down, Daisy.'

She swallowed quietly and pulled out the short wooden seat, lowering herself down before looking up. Mrs Goodyear took a box of Kleenex from her desk drawers, placing it in front of her.

'Daisy, I'm afraid I have some bad news. Your mother has been in a terrible car accident. Your father rang from the hospital. He has organised for one of your neighbours to come and collect you who should be arriving shortly to take you to the hospital.'

Daisy's head spun. Had she heard right? Her mum? An accident?

But before she had a moment more to let it sink in, Mrs Goodyear stood up as there was a knock at the door.

'Oh, Daisy,' said a familiar voice. 'I'm so sorry, love.'

Geoff from two door's down stood in the doorway, his massive physique filling the frame.

'Mr. Smeeton?'

Geoff nodded. 'Aye,' he said as Daisy slowly lifted herself from the chair, bending back down to collect her school bag.

'Daisy, take all the time you need. I'll speak to your father over the next few days to sort things out.'

She nodded, her eyes glazed, not understanding what was happening. Why couldn't her father have come for her?

'Come on, my love. I'll get you to the hospital as soon as possible,' said Geoff, in his broad Yorkshire accent.

oOo

'Dad?'

'Daisy?'

She rushed into his arms, and he began to sob uncontrollably.

'Oh Daisy, Daisy,' he cried over and over again.

'Dad? Can I see her? Can I see Mum?'

Beau Madigan pulled away from his only daughter and looked down into her intense green eyes. She looked so much like her mother; he thought before he nodded and led her through the ICU. The smell turned her stomach. She didn't quite understand it at the time, but it smelled like death.

The moment she turned the corner and spotted her beautiful mother, Daisy let out a cry.

'Mum,' she sobbed, rushing to her side, almost falling to her knees beside the bed.

Her mother was only really recognisable by the tufts of bright red curly hair that stuck out from the bandage across her head. Her mouth and nose were full of tubes and where her usually happy freckled face should be was a swollen, pale bruised one instead.

Beau stood behind his daughter as tears poured down his cheeks.

'I should be able to do something,' he said. 'I should be able to help. That's what I do. I'm a protector,' he muttered over and over again.

Turning to look at her dad, Daisy grabbed his hand, 'What? You couldn't do anything, Dad. It's not your fault.'

Beau momentarily glanced at her, but his eyes appeared to glaze over. 'No, my job. It was a protector. I should have protected her, and now it's too late.'

'Dad? What are you talking about? It's not too late. She's going to get better. Mum's going to be fine.'

'Mr Madigan, please could you and your daughter move to the waiting room? We need some space in here,' said a petite young woman wearing scrubs.

Beau bent down and placed a gentle kiss on his wife's cheek, whispering something into her ear. But before Daisy knew what had happened, he'd rushed from the room, leaving her to go and sit in the waiting room alone.

Leaning back against the green coloured wall, Daisy closed her eyes, trying to get the image of her mum out of her mind. She remembered what she'd looked like earlier that morning when she'd left for school. All smiley, smelling of Daisy perfume (which Beau had bought for her 35th birthday just a week ago) with her long curly hair half tied up. She was beautiful. Daisy smiled. She wanted to remember that image, nothing else.

'Daisy?'

Opening her eyes, she turned to face her mother. 'Mum!'

Sitting beside her was the beautiful woman who had raised her, looking just as she had earlier that day.

'Mum... I don't understand.'

Esther Madigan smiled and reached out to gently stroke her daughter's cheek.

Daisy felt her warmth but not her touch.

'I want you to know how much I love you and your father. You mean the world to me and I'm so sorry that I have to leave you...'

'Mum, no,' whispered Daisy with a quivering bottom lip. 'You can't go. You're just a little banged up from the accident, that's all. You're going to be fine.'

But Esther shook her head, 'No, Daisy. My body couldn't take it. I need you to be strong for you and your dad, okay? You can get through this. I may not be here in body, but I will always be with you,' she said as she hovered her hand above Daisy's heart.

'Mum... please don't do this. Please don't go. Mum, I love you so much. We can't live without you.'

'Shhhh,' whispered Esther, 'Yes, you can. You're special, Daisy. I know Beau and I always told you that, and you never believed us but you are. Very special. You got that from your father. You share something, the two of you. And something big is going to happen very soon. When it does, I need you to be strong. It's your destiny, Daisy,' Esther smiled as she slowly began to fade, her body becoming more and more transparent.

'Mum? Mum! No!' yelled Daisy grappling after her.

'Be strong, Daisy. Remember, I will always love you, your father too. Goodbye, my angel.'

Sobbing as she'd never sobbed before, Daisy could barely catch her breath as she listened to the doctors and nurses frantically working down the corridor, presumably trying to save the now life-less body of her mother.

\## 2

Her dad had disappeared. Daisy was alone in every sense of
the word.

She'd walked all the way home in the rain. Soaked to
the bone, she pushed open the front door, hoping to find him
there. But there was nothing but a cold empty house. The warmth
she'd always felt upon entering had vanished. Daisy leaned against
the wall in the hallway and slid to the soft, carpeted floor. A loud
cry erupted from her lips as the sobbing began again. She'd never
experienced pain like it. She felt like her heart had been ripped
from her chest, leaving just a gaping hole, and the feeling of being
asphyxiated.

'Mum, oh Mum,' she cried, her breath coming in short, sharp
bursts.

Daylight began to disappear slowly and darkness set in while
Daisy remained curled up at the foot of the stairs listening to the
ticking of the clock in the kitchen. She heard faint voices as neighbours began to arrive home from school and work. Life went on as
usual for the rest of the world, but not for Daisy.

Eventually, shivering with cold and still in wet clothes, she
forced herself up. Clinging to the bannister, Daisy finally stood up
and removed her coat, letting it fall to the floor.

Mum will get angry with me at leaving wet clothes on the floor;

she suddenly thought as she bent to pick it up. But she's not here any more She's gone. She's dead.

She bawled her eyes out again as she slowly climbed the stairs, taking off the rest of her wet clothes, throwing them into the linen basket in the bathroom.

Turning on the shower, she let the steam fill the room before stepping under the hot water, hoping that it might ease away the tension that filled her every pore.

oOo

LATER THAT NIGHT, AFTER DAISY HAD CLIMBED INTO HER BED IN her warmest pyjamas, she'd fallen asleep quickly. But the sound of a door slamming downstairs startled her out of slumber.

For a split second, all was well.

'Mum?' she whispered.

But suddenly she was kicked violently in the stomach as the memory of earlier returned with a vengeance. Wincing in emotional pain, Daisy let out a gasp as tears began to fall.

Turning back the covers, she climbed out of bed and tiptoed to look over the railing.

The lamp in the hall had been switched on.

'Dad?' she asked as she walked down the stairs and into the living room. She found him sprawled on the floor, a near-empty bottle of vodka falling out of his outstretched hand.

She rushed to his side, 'Dad?' she said, trying to shake him out of his stupor. 'Dad, can you hear me?'

He murmured something unintelligible before he began snoring.

Not knowing what to do, Daisy took the bottle away, emptying the remnants of vodka down the sink, before finding a blanket to place over him. She then lay down on the sofa with a framed photo of the three of them clutched to her chest before closing her eyes.

❈ 3 ❈

'Happy 15th Birthday, Daisy,' she whispered to herself five weeks later as she woke up to find her dad in a drunken stupor on the bathroom floor. His sweatshirt was lifted slightly to reveal a tattoo on his lower back. Daisy had always loved that image of the eye with the wings and the Latin words beneath.

Closing her eyes for a moment, she took a deep breath and counted to ten. When she re-opened them, she stepped in and tried to wake him.

'Dad... wake up. Come on. You've got to stop drinking. Mum would hate to see you like this. I hate to see you like this.'

But Beau said nothing. He was out cold.

Tutting, she stepped back over him and went downstairs. At least they had a downstairs toilet.

Her birthdays had always been a great cause for celebration. The moment Daisy woke up until the moment she put her head back on the pillow, Beau and Esther had surprised her with gifts, fun and games, outings and parties for three.

This year would be the first year, unlike any other.

Her mum had gone and so, in a manner of speaking, had her dad.

She'd returned to school a week after her mum had died. The kids stopped taunting her, and she felt utterly invisible once again.

But Daisy would have chosen to be the victim of all the bullying in the world if it meant she could have her mum back.

Three weeks after her death, Daisy had stopped going to school altogether. Her dad was in a bad way, and she was the only person who could look out for him.

Not even Geoff from two doors down could help because he'd had to move back to Yorkshire to look after an elderly relative. They had no other family and no other friends. It had always been just the three of them, and that had worked out wonderfully until, well, until it became only the two of them.

Opening the fridge door, she found it to be empty, so she looked around the house for her dad's wallet. Opening it, she found a few measly pounds.

'Dad, we need to get some supplies. There's nothing to eat, and we need to eat. Dad, can you give me some money so I can go out and get something?'

He lay motionless on the floor.

Frustrated, she kicked out at the wall, 'For God's Sake, Dad!'

He groaned and rolled over.

Running back downstairs, she opened the front door, slamming it behind her.

Arriving at the local corner shop, she bought what she could, which was milk and bread. Tears began to fall down her cheeks as she paid silently. Walking slowly back up the road, she winced at a pain in her foot.

Great, now what? She thought as she hobbled slightly. Stopping for a moment, she wiggled her toes, bending her ankle this way and that but the pain persevered. She limped back to the house, where she toasted a couple of slices of bread and ate it with a cup of sweet milky tea.

The pain in her foot seemed to have moved, making its way up her ankle to her calf. She rubbed it absent-mindedly

The sound of a door slamming startled her.

'Dad?' she shouted, running through the hall. She opened the front door to see him climbing into his old Fiat. He drove off without a backward glance.

'Dad? No!' she yelled, 'You're so drunk,' she whispered, crying. He could kill himself driving that car and then it would be just me.

Maybe that's what he wants. Maybe he doesn't care about me. Maybe he just wants to be with Mum.

Daisy walked back into the living room, where she sat quietly staring at the wall for two hours. Flashbacks of her life before continued to run through her mind. The times she sat at her mum's dressing table as Esther carefully combed her daughter's curls; Saturday mornings in the kitchen preparing a special breakfast of golden pancakes; days out on the coast, walking along the beach eating ice cream; visits to their favourite castle in Sussex; cold evenings in, the three of them curled up under a blanket on the sofa watching TV shows...

Intense, agonising pain in her lower back doubled her over, and she cried out in shock.

Curled on the floor, she winced as the pain seemed to come and go in waves.

When she was finally able to stand up, she rushed to her bedroom. She opened her wardrobe door and stood in front of the full-length mirror and gingerly lifted her top, gasping at what she saw.

There etched into her lower back was what looked like a tattoo. It wasn't easy to see it correctly from that angle, but Daisy was sure it was a big eye with wings and beneath the image were words. But she couldn't read them in the reflection.

But none of that worried her at that moment because she'd seen it before. Her father had the same tattoo on his lower back.

❦   4   ❦

Acouple of hours later, Beau returned home on foot. He didn't say a word. He just dropped a couple of hundred pounds on the coffee table in front of her before turning to walk away.

'Dad? Dad, please talk to me. It's been weeks now. Mum wouldn't want this to go on, she, she...' the words struggled to come out of her mouth as she watched her father from behind. His shoulders slumped forward as he stopped and listened.

He turned, and she caught her breath as she saw his tear-filled eyes. But he could barely look at her.

'Dad... please,' she begged, standing up. 'I need you now...' she sobbed, but Beau couldn't take it. With his lips quivering, he shook his head and turned away.

Daisy fell back onto the sofa and let the tears fall down her cheeks as she heard the front door slam. She listened to the sound of his footsteps as he walked down the road.

After about an hour, she stood up, took the money and walked upstairs. The pain in her back returned and reminded her of the strange etching that had appeared there. Stripping down to her underwear, she stood in front of the mirror once again, stretching, trying to read the words. How had it appeared there? What was it? How could someone have tattooed her without her knowing about it? It was impossible. She wished she could ask her dad, but she knew now that wasn't going to happen. He could barely look at her, let alone talk to her.

Reaching into her desk drawer, she pulled out the orange coloured camera she'd got for Christmas a year earlier. With some difficulty, she managed to take a snapshot of her back. Pulling on her jeans and sweater, she then placed the memory card into her laptop and clicked on the image.

The tattoo was identical to her father's. The only difference was the words placed beneath it. Hers read Semper Fidelis while her father's had something completely different, not that she could remember now.

A knock on the front door made her jump. Her first instinct was to hide. Since her mum had died, she hated having to talk to people, so she tiptoed to her window and gingerly peered out. Two men stood patiently waiting as they knocked for a second time.

When one of them looked upwards, Daisy flattened herself against the wall, holding the blue velvet curtain over her face.

After a few more minutes, she watched them as they shrugged and walked away. They climbed back into their car and drove away.

Rushing downstairs, she crouched to pick up the letter they'd pushed through the letterbox. Opening it, she gasped. They were being evicted from their home. The house where she'd grown up. Where would they go? What would happen to her?

Later that night as she sat curled up in front of the TV, the electricity went off. Not because of a problem down the line or anything like that. No, it was because they hadn't paid their bill.

She stood up angrily and kicked at the coffee table. To her amazement, the table lifted high up and crashed through the wall, into the dining room.

As she stood still, her face went white as she realised the destruction she'd caused. But moments later, she lifted the tall glass vase, the one her mum had always filled with a bunch of daisies every Saturday morning and hurled it at the wall, shattering it into tiny pieces. Next, without even thinking, she picked up the television like it was a piece of cardboard and tossed it through the same hole in the wall, smashing it to the dining room floor.

She tore the beige velvet curtains from their pole and sat, ripping them apart as if they were nothing but pieces of paper. The simple act of making a horrendous mess somehow made her feel better, albeit temporarily. But she continued her trail of destruction until the entire bottom floor of the house looked like a tornado had hit it.

Standing at the foot of the stairs, Daisy surveyed the mess she'd made before her knees buckled beneath her.

'Mum... I'm sorry. I'm so sorry, Mum. I'm just so, so angry. I don't know what to do. Where are we going to go? Oh, Mum, why did you leave us?'

Some hours later, curled on the floor in the darkness of the late afternoon, Daisy watched as a tiny light in the distance began to slowly move towards her, becoming brighter and brighter until she had to shield her eyes with her arm.

'Daisy?' whispered a voice.

'Y..yes?'

'Daisy, dear, it's me. Nanna.'

'Nanna?'

Daisy removed her arm and lifted her upper body off of the floor so that she sat cross-legged looking into the light.

'Yes, dear, your Nanna. Oh, deary me, whatever has happened here, my love? I know you're feeling angry, but this is no way to handle it. You mustn't take out your anger on things like this... or people, my dear. You must learn to channel that anger. You're so strong, my dear. You're just like your mother in that respect. And that's why you need to pull yourself together. You need to look after your father. Beau is a good man, Daisy. He just can't take the pain. He can't take the loss. Your dear mother was like his backbone, and he's lost, so very lost without her. You must be strong, Daisy. You must help him through this. It's the only way you'll be able to help yourself through this.'

'Nanna?'

'Yes, dear?'

'Is Mum with you? Can I speak to her?'

Daisy watched the light as it began to lose its sparkle. The faint outline of her grandmother appearing in front of her.

'Now, Daisy. Your mother is resting with all of the family that went before her. She's not quite strong enough to see you or your father. She wanted to, of course, she wanted to, but we didn't feel it was a good idea. Not right now. Not yet, my dear. It's too soon.'

Daisy's bottom lip quivered.

'Now now, my dear. I know you're sad, but you must understand that you will see her again. At some stage, we will all be together again. But now is not that time, do you understand?'

Daisy slowly nodded.

'But Nanna. How can I see you? Are you real? Am I dreaming?'

Her grandmother smiled and held out her hand. Daisy felt a warm feeling on her cheek, the same kind of warm feeling she'd got when her mother had touched her.

'You're not dreaming, my dear. I had to come and reassure you that all will be alright, eventually as long as you stay strong. You're an extraordinary girl, Daisy and I believe you've already received a sign about that. It comes from your father's side of the family, my dear. At some point, you will understand what it's all about and why you have it.'

'What Nanna? What are you talking about?'

'Semper Fidelis, my dear, Semper Fidelis.'

And then Daisy was alone again, curled up at the foot of the stairs in the darkness.

❧   5   ❧

The following day, Daisy escaped to the only other place she ever felt safe: Abney Park.

Abney Park was a vast former cemetery that had been left to become overgrown over the years. Some people used it to walk their dogs during the day, and for others, it was a place to escape from their busy day to day lives. Though many others kept their distance as the area was also known to be creepy, frightening and possibly even haunted.

To Daisy, it felt like home. There were plenty of hiding places that few others knew about. She could stay there for hours on end and not come across a single person.

Sitting beneath her favourite statue, one of a sleeping lion, Daisy opened her sketchbook and began to draw. Soon the image of a beautiful woman with a contagious smile began to look back at her. Daisy stopped what she was doing and just looked at the picture before tearing the page out of the book and screwing it up, tossing it to her side with a silent scream. The piece of paper began to blow away in the wind, hopping along in the dirt and settling between two ancient headstones metres away from where she sat.

She tried to ignore it, but seconds later, Daisy scrambled to her feet and rushed over, tripping and falling in the process, knocking her knee on the gravestone.

'Ouch!'

'Oh, are you alright?' said a voice that nearly scared her half to death.

Grabbing the picture and shoving it into her pocket, Daisy turned to see who the voice belonged to. A guy about a couple of years older than her stood leaning casually on the lion. He reminded her of that guy from Oliver Twist; you know the one that takes Oliver under his wing. Cheeky-looking and a bit scary.

Daisy gulped and turned to run away.

'Don't go,' he yelled. 'I didn't mean to startle you.'

His voice, all tender and gentle, didn't match his face.

Daisy guiltily turned, her cheeks reddening as she stopped walking.

'I... I saw you drawing and wanted to talk but,' he shrugged his shoulders and smiled a lop-sided grin. Stepping forward toward her, he brushed his long dark fringe to one side and said, 'I'm Jack.'

Daisy smiled. The Artful Dodger, that's who he reminded her of, and his real name was Jack too.

'Daisy,' she answered, standing still.

'You're a good artist,' he said, pointing to her sketchbook.

Daisy shook her head, shyly, 'not really,' she whispered.

But he nodded vigorously, 'You are... honestly.'

She smiled.

'So... what are you doing here all on your own?'

This time, Daisy was the one to shrug.

'That's okay if you'd rather not say. I get it,' he said sadly.

'I really should go,' Daisy said. 'My... erm... Dad's waiting for me.'

Jack smiled, 'Yeh, okay. Maybe I'll see you around... Daisy.'

She reddened, nodded and turned, running away as fast as she could.

Within minutes, Daisy stood outside her home. The home that wouldn't be home for much longer. Taking a deep breath, she slid the key into the lock and walked inside. Her dad sat on the bottom step of the stairs.

'Daisy?' he whispered.

The shock of hearing him speak made her drop the keys. Leaning forward to pick them up, she said nothing, just waited to see what he had to say for himself.

'We have to leave,' he stuttered. He didn't mention the almighty mess she'd made. Perhaps he understood.

'I know. I saw the letter.'

She watched him struggle to speak.

'Where are we going to go?' she asked.

He gulped hard, 'I... I don't...' he croaked, 'I don't know, love.'

He hadn't called her 'love' in such a long time that she felt a lump in her throat.

'Do we have any money?'

Beau slowly shook his head.

'You mean, you and mum never saved anything up?'

He looked embarrassed.

'But why? What about me, Dad? Did you never think about me?'

She was angry.

'Daisy, I know... I know you're angry. I'm angry too. I never thought this would happen. I always thought we would be okay the way we were.'

'You should have planned for emergencies, Dad. You never know what's going to happen in life. I, I thought you and Mum were better prepared than this. This is crazy. So we don't have any money, we don't have anywhere to go. You don't have a job now that you're drunk all the time. What are we going to do? Dad, answer me that? Oh, and while you're actually talking to me, perhaps you can explain this too,' she shouted as she turned around and lifted her sweatshirt to reveal the tattoo inked into her back.

When Beau saw it, he gasped loudly.

'But, you're only 15,' he stuttered. 'It's not supposed to happen until you're 16.'

'What Dad? What is it? And why shouldn't it happen until I'm 16?'

Beau stood up to take a closer look.

'Semper Fidelis,' he said with a sad smile. 'I should have known.'

'But what is it, Dad? I don't understand?'

Beau's eyebrows knitted together as he turned his daughter back around, placing a hand on her shoulders, Daisy saw a tear slide down his cheek.

'I'm sorry, Daisy. But this is all happening at the wrong time. You don't deserve any of this. You deserve a much better father than me. I'm so very sorry. You're better off without me. Now that I know you've developed already. I know you can get on with your life. I know you're going to be alright. You're so strong, in more ways than you know. You will get through this, and you shouldn't have to do it with a drunken father to deal with. You'll manage, Daisy. I promise you that.'

The last few words came out in sobs.

'But Dad,' she whispered. 'I don't understand.'

'We have to be out of the house by tomorrow afternoon. You're going to be alright, Daisy,' he said sadly. Leaning forward, he gently kissed her forehead and then before she knew what had happened, the front door was open and he'd gone. Again. But this time it felt final. Daisy knew he'd left for good. She knew she was now on her own.

❦ 6 ❦

She still had the money from the sale of the car that she tucked carefully into her bra top. All her treasured belongings were folded and placed into the large rucksack that she hiked onto her back. As she stepped through the front door, she took a long look backwards, wiping her eyes roughly with the back of her fingerless gloved hand and closed the door behind her.

She knew precisely where she would go. It was her second home, after all.

Walking through the old wrought iron gates, she almost felt like she was being welcomed home. For the first time in weeks, Daisy smiled, took a long deep breath and stepped over the threshold into Abney Park.

Taking her usual route, she followed the well-worn pathway until she reached the old lion, as she liked to call him. When she got there, she gently stroked his sleeping face and let her rucksack fall to the floor beside her. She even did a little twirl before falling onto her bottom with a sigh.

Laying backwards onto the moss-covered ground, Daisy looked upwards at the patchy blue sky, watching as cloud after cloud scattered past in a hurry. The tall trees swayed in the breeze as if dancing to a silent overture. Daisy began to imagine what they could be dancing to as she watched intently how they started to move more slowly across the sky. Soon she was humming along, trying to match the song to the movements, like a family game she remembered from Christmas time where they would take it in turns to hum a song and the others would have to guess what song it was. Daisy smiled as she remembered how good a voice her dad had. He was such a fantastic singer. He could quite easily have done that for a living if he wasn't always so drunk these days.

Unkeen to think about her father, Daisy returned her attention to the potential sounds of the dancing trees. Ultimately choosing Coldplay's Paradise as the perfect song. With her eyes now closed, Daisy sang quietly along:

'Para-para-paradise, Para-para-paradise, Para-para-paradise...'

'It sounds like you're singing about yourself... Daisy,' said a familiar voice, making her jump up in fear.

'Jesus!' she yelped at the same time.

'Oh... there I go again, frightening the life out of you. Sorry,' Jack said blushing.

'Do you mind if I sit down?' he asked politely.

Eyeing him up and down, Daisy decided she had no choice. It's not like she owned the park.

'Sure,' she said, moving her bag out of his way.

'You're an amazing singer,' he offered.

Daisy spluttered, knowing very well that he was lying because she'd always thought she sounded terrible when she tried to sing. Her mum had always cringed and laughed.

'Then you must be tone-deaf because I can't sing.'

He looked at her with an odd expression.

'I ain't tone-deaf, and I'm telling you, you can sing. I'd go so far as to say your singing is even better than your drawing and that's saying something.'

Daisy laughed, 'I think you must be on something, then.'

'Actually, I'm a musician myself, so I know when someone can sing.'

'Whatever,' said Daisy before realising how rude that sounded. 'Sorry,' she added, lowering her eyes to the ground.

'S'okay. What are you doing here, anyway? You look like a runaway or something?'

Daisy shrugged her shoulders.

Jack held up his hands, 'Still not ready to talk then? No problem.'

Daisy felt even guiltier. She had been brought up to be polite and friendly, and here she was rude and unfriendly.

'Look, I'm sorry... it's just a long, complicated story, that's all.'

'Well, Daisy,' he said as he leaned back on to his elbow, 'I've got all the time in the world.'

✻ 7 ✻

It was the first time Daisy had ever had a real friend. Crazy, considering she was now 15. She'd always felt different from the other kids at school, and it never really helped when most of them at that place had been so horrible to her. In the end, she'd just decided she was a loner, at least at school, anyway. Away from school, she had never needed any friends because she was so close to her mum and dad. The thought choked her up, and she tried to push them from her mind. She didn't want to cry again. She'd spent so much time crying over the past few months that she felt all cried out.

Turning over in the darkness, Daisy shivered as she watched the nearly full moon through the hole in the roof. She zipped the sleeping bag up tighter around her face and watched a slither of cloud momentarily darken the world around her. When the moon appeared again, she sighed, rolling over on to her side and closed her eyes.

She'd been sleeping in the dilapidated old chapel for just over two months, and it was getting colder, but it was the only place she could find that wasn't wholly open to the elements. She'd gotten by okay until then, but the last of her money would soon run out and then what would she do? She'd had no choice but to buy herself a decent sleeping bag and some other 'camping' equipment to allow her to continue to live outdoors, but the lack of funds was beginning to worry her. She fell asleep, wondering how she would feed herself.

The following morning, Daisy woke up to find Jack sitting a few metres away, watching her.

'Hey,' she yawned. 'What are you doing here? Shouldn't you be in school?'

'It's Sunday, Daisy,' he laughed, throwing a stone in her direction.

'Oh, right,' she said as she climbed out of the sleeping bag and shivered slightly. It was starting to get a little chilly.

'Are you okay, Daisy?'

She nodded, folding it and shoving it back into her rucksack with the rest of her worldly possessions.

'Why do you ask?'

'Well, it's seriously cold now. I don't know how you're coping with all this.'

'I'm coping fine thank you very much. I can look after myself,' she said with her chin jutting out in front of her.

Jack frowned, 'Daisy... you can't go on like this.'

'Course I can,' she sulked. 'Besides, where am I supposed to go? What am I supposed to do? I'm 15, Jack. I can look after myself just fine. Just... just mind your own business.'

Her face flushed a deep red colour as she realised she was having her first argument with her only friend. She didn't like it. But when she turned back to apologise, he'd gone.

'Great,' she muttered under her breath before plonking herself down on the stone floor. She held her head in her hands and shook it. Tears threatened to erupt, but she knocked them back, refusing to cry. She never wanted to cry again, about anything.

Taking a piece of stale bread out of her bag, she stood up, put the bag on her back and walked out of the chapel into the crisp fresh air. She took a bite, chewed for a few moments and tried hard to swallow what tasted like a piece of cardboard. It was gross. But it was all she had, and she didn't want to spend her last few pounds, not yet anyway.

Walking through the cemetery, she shied away from the early morning joggers, dog walkers and photographers keen to take advantage of the light. She felt like her space was being invaded, but it was the same every Sunday morning at Abney Park.

Everywhere she went, she spotted a stranger wandering about, and she wanted to scream at them to go away. But it didn't belong to her. She knew that deep down.

So she decided to take a walk away from the park. As she strolled through the large open gates that led away from the vast forested green space, her heart began to race, and she felt nervous. But she held her head up high and carried on walking along the road as cars sped by beside her.

Crossing at the traffic lights, she spotted a small corner shop with fruit and veg on a stall outside. Her mouth watered as she remembered the flavours of those juicy apples. She could even smell them as she moved closer and closer until she stood directly in front of the stall. Sweet and tangy, the memory filled her mouth as it began to water. Before she'd even given it a single thought, Daisy swiped an apple and took a long hard bite, the juices dripping down her chin.

'Oy, you better be planning on paying for that,' shouted an angry looking Indian man who'd appeared from nowhere.

Daisy, startled, swallowed it and turned to run. Her heartbeat increased, and before she knew what she'd done, she was back at the cemetery in a matter of seconds.

Confused at the speed in which she'd run home, Daisy checked to make sure nobody was following her and rushed back through the gates, looking for a hidden spot where she could sit and try to make sense of what had just happened.

As she settled down onto the moss-covered ground in a corner hidden from view, Daisy looked at the bitten apple in her hand guiltily.

I stole it, she thought. I've never taken a single thing. Mum would be so mad.

Soon, the tears she'd been trying to keep at bay flooded through her tear ducts as she sobbed her heart out. 'I'm not a thief,' she whispered, shaking her head.

An outstretched hand patted her gently on her shoulder. Daisy didn't even look up as Jack took a seat by her side. She knew it was him. Since they'd become friends, she always knew when he was near. She could somehow feel his presence.

'I stole it, Jack,' she sobbed, as he carefully put his arm across her, pulling her into him. She dropped her head onto his shoulder, and they quietly sat as Daisy sobbed until there were no more tears to cry.

'I'm sorry about earlier,' she eventually whispered.

Jack hugged her tighter, and she knew he didn't mind.

'Come on,' he said a bit later as he stood and held out his hand to help her up.

'Where to?' she asked.

'My parents are out for the day... I thought you might like to take a shower.'

Daisy's face lit up, 'Really?'

He laughed and nodded.

8

Daisy returned to the corner shop a week later to apologise to the older man. She handed him her last few coins but, just as he was about to take it, he looked at her face for a moment. Then he curled her fingers over the coins and smiled.

'What is your name, child?'

'D..D..aisy.'

'Daisy, you have a good heart,' and with that, he turned and walked back into the shop.

She was stumped. She looked left, then right and walked in behind him, swallowing hard.

'Daisy, I can see you have fallen on hard times, and that is not easy when you are so young. I have a proposition for you...'

With her eyes wide open, she smiled shyly, 'Erm... yes?'

'If you come here every Sunday to help me out in the shop, I will pay you in food.'

Her eyes lit up with the possibility of earning some food, and she grinned like a little child. 'Yes, please,' she exclaimed. 'I would love to do that! Thank you, thank you so much.'

'You can start today. But first, come and meet my wife.'

Daisy followed him through the back of the store and up some stairs until she stood in a cosy apartment filled with the delicious smells of Indian spices. Her stomach rumbled, and she blushed.

'Balvinder, there is someone here I'd like you to meet,' said the old man.

A tiny elderly lady walked into the living room with a kind face and smile.

'Hello,' she said brightly, holding out her hand.

Daisy moved forward and shook her hand, 'I'm Daisy,' she whispered shyly.

'Who?' she answered loudly.

'You'll have to speak up, Daisy. Balvinder doesn't hear as well as she used to.'

'I'm Daisy,' she repeated loudly.

'Crazy?'

Daisy giggled, 'No, Daisy.'

'Maisie?'

Daisy repressed a laugh, 'Daisy.'

'Ah... Daisy. Nice to meet you, Daisy,' she smiled before turning to her husband, expectantly.

'Daisy is going to help out downstairs every Sunday... in return for some food.'

Balvinder's eyebrows knitted together and she shrugged, turning back to Daisy. 'Okay,' she smiled, then she sniffed and grimaced, moving closer to her.

'You need to bathe?' she asked.

Daisy blushed from head to toe and nodded sheepishly.

'Okay, you bathe here every week before you go to work. Otherwise... no work!' said Balvinder as she helped the teenager out of her coat. 'Follow me,' she said, leaving her husband to return downstairs.

Daisy did as she was told, giving her clothes to the old lady. 'I'll wash these,' she said as she held them at arm's length.

Later that day, Daisy felt better than she had done in ages. Those wonderful people had befriended her and offered her everything that she needed — food, bathing facilities once a week and a little work. At the end of the day, Balvinder had even given her a home-cooked meal to take with her. Her husband, Shariq had handed her a plastic bag full of food that would last her until next Sunday. Daisy hugged them both and waved goodbye as she ran back to Abney Park. She couldn't wait to tell Jack what had happened, but it would probably have to wait until tomorrow.

That night as Daisy slept in the old chapel, she awoke with a start. A terrible feeling engulfed her, and she hugged her knees to her chest tightly. She didn't know why, but tears began to fall down her cheeks slowly. Something had happened, something awful.

'Jack,' she whispered. She could feel his presence again. 'What are you doing here? Its the middle of the night,' she asked as she sat upright and searched for him in the darkness.

'Where are you?' she asked. 'Jack? I know you're here.'

But Jack didn't show himself. Confusion filled her head as she climbed out of the sleeping bag. Jack. Something had happened to Jack. She just knew it. She quickly fumbled with her bag, throwing it on her back before rushing out of the chapel. She ran as fast as she could out of the park towards his house. She remembered the way from two weeks ago.

As she got closer and closer, the smell of smoke filled her nostrils, and Daisy's sense of foreboding became stronger and stronger.

'Jack!' she yelled as she turned the street corner to find a scene of utter devastation. Several fire engines stood parked right outside Jack's house, now a burning building. She could hear cries and shrieks as neighbours gathered on the pavement on the opposite side of the road. People sobbed as an ambulance screeched away from the curb and down the road.

'Jack?' Daisy sobbed. She knew he was in that ambulance so she raced down the road and followed it to the hospital, running as fast as she could, without ever losing her breath.

When she arrived, she watched as the ambulance door was flung open and the stretcher pulled out. She rushed forward as the team from the hospital took over, taking Jack inside, into the A&E.

As Daisy stepped forward into the emergency room, she suddenly couldn't breathe. A memory she'd pushed so back into her mind had re-surfaced, and she suddenly remembered that day she'd arrived at the same hospital to find her mother at death's door.

Intense pain like it was yesterday clutched at her chest, but she broke through, made herself breathe again – for Jack. She needed to see Jack.

'No, sorry. You can't go in there,' said a friendly face.

'But... but he's my best friend. I need to make sure he's okay. I need to see him. Please, please let me see him.'

The nurse smiled sadly and shook her head, 'I'm sorry, you need to let the doctors help him right now. Why don't you sit down over there and I'll keep you updated on his condition? Perhaps later, okay?' she smiled.

Daisy clutched at her chest, the pain was intolerable, but she did as she was told.

Nodding, she turned away from the nurse and walked towards the waiting room, the same waiting room where her mother had said goodbye. She couldn't say goodbye to Jack too. She just couldn't.

'He's going to be fine. He's going to be fine,' Daisy muttered to herself over and over as she took a seat and pulled her knees close to her chest.

She'd lost her mother, lost her father and now maybe she would lose her best friend too. What had she done to deserve this?

As she lifted her eyes from the floor, she looked around. There were loads of people wandering around the corridors. Some looked lost and sad. But there were also a few nurses who looked odd. Daisy watched them as they stood chatting to each other, occasionally walking into another room. But it was their manner of dress that wasn't quite right. In fact, it was downright weird. They looked like were from another time.

Long white dresses with starched white collars and frilly caps. Had they come from a fancy dress party? And then, just when she thought it couldn't get any more bizarre, a man appeared wearing blue tights, an extravagant red coat that cinched in at the waist, a frilly white shirt beneath it and a large hat. Daisy rubbed her eyes and looked back at him in amazement. The man turned to look at her, nodded his head and carried on walking, right through the wall.

Daisy lost her breath again. She sat bolt upright then put her fingers to her lips, about to gnaw on her nails when the friendly nurse appeared again.

'I'm sorry, but it doesn't look too good. If you come with me, I can smuggle you in but just for a moment, okay?'

Daisy forgot all about the odd characters wandering around the hospital and stood up, quickly following behind the sweet nurse. As she walked into the cubicle, an involuntary sob burst from her lips.

'Jack,' she muttered as she stepped forward to see him. He was deathly pale. It was then than she knew she was going to lose him.

'I don't understand.'

The nurse stepped forward, 'there was just too much smoke inhalation, I'm afraid. We don't think he'll make it through the night. I'm so sorry. Perhaps you should say goodbye now.'

Daisy's bottom lip quivered, 'No, I won't say goodbye. I can't.'

The nurse looked on sadly, 'I'll give you a couple of minutes.'

'Wait... what happened to his family. His mum and dad?'

The nurse shook her head, 'he was the only one to make it out alive. I'm so sorry.'

Daisy gingerly sat on the bed and placed her hand over Jack's.

'Please don't die, Jack. Please don't leave me. I can't lose you as well.'

She sat with her eyes closed and her head on his bed for ten minutes.

'Daisy?' said a familiar voice.

Sitting bolt upright, Daisy let out a deep sigh. 'I knew you wouldn't die. I knew you'd make it,' she smiled with utter relief.

But Jack looked the same, with his eyes closed. He looked peaceful.

'Jack?' she asked.

'Daisy? I'm here,' said the voice.

Daisy slowly turned her head until she saw him standing at the foot of the bed. He stood looking over at his own body sadly.

'No,' she whispered, 'Not you too. Jack no, it's not fair. Don't go, don't leave me. Please, please, no,' she cried, sobbing loudly until the nurse appeared once again. She approached the bed and checked his vital signs, but he'd gone.

'I'm sorry, my love, but he's gone. Come on; it's better that you go now,' she said as she carefully placed the sheet over his face.

Daisy looked around the room, but there was no sign of Jack.

She sobbed and ran out of the room, out of the hospital, running flat out until she arrived at the cemetery. She could barely see for the tears blurred her vision. But she kept on running until she arrived at the old chapel and threw herself on to the floor, gasping for air and sobbing loudly.

'Shhhh Daisy, don't cry.'

'Jack? You're still here?' she asked, looking around in confusion.

'I'm here, Daisy, I'm here,' and her friend walked towards her from the darkened corner of the nave.

She stood up and rushed towards him, wanting to hold him tight, but she walked right through him, stumbling and falling to the ground, banging her knee as she did so.

'I'm sorry Daisy. I wish I could hold you, but I can't. I'm, I'm...dead.'

The tears began again as she sobbed loudly and shook her head. Her whole body trembled.

'Daisy, I won't leave you, I promise I won't leave you.'

Daisy's tears began to dry a little as she turned to look at his ghost.

'You won't?'

Jack shook his head.

'Now take out your sleeping bag and get inside. Get warm. It will make you feel better, I promise.'

Daisy did as he asked and curled up inside her sleeping bag. She felt the warmth creep up her body until, eventually, the trembling stopped.

'There,' he said, 'that's better isn't it?'

She nodded as he lay down beside her, so they were facing each other.

'I'm sorry, Jack. I'm sorry about your parents.'

Jack smiled sadly, 'I guess it was our time to go.'

'What happened?'

'I don't know. I don't remember it. I remember my parents coming to me in the hospital after you'd gone. They looked so peaceful and happy. I never saw them look like that before. They walked into the light.'

'But why didn't you go with them?'

'I told them I would meet them over there. I told them I couldn't leave you, not yet.'

Daisy lifted her head, 'thank you,' she sniffed, and he smiled.

They lay like that until her breathing slowed, and Jack was sure she was asleep. And then he disappeared.

9

For the next month, Jack never left her side. He called himself her 'guardian angel', or 'guardian ghost'. Although he'd died that night in the house fire, Daisy never felt like she had truly lost him. He made sure of that.

He even went with her to Balvinder and Shariq's corner shop every Sunday. But it wasn't easy being around other people because they couldn't see Jack. Daisy was the only person who could.

She'd told him of her experience in the hospital – her mum who'd appeared shortly after her death, the strange-looking nurses and the man dressed like someone from centuries ago. Jack had returned to the hospital and found that, sure enough, those nurses and several oddly-dressed men frequently floated through the building. He had tried to talk to them, but they said they were too busy.

So Daisy could see ghosts; it was as simple as that.

'But why did I only see them in the hospital? And why you?' she asked one day while they were wandering about the cemetery reading people's headstones from many years ago. 'Why can't I see ghosts around here? I mean, this is a cemetery, there must be loads around here?'

Jack shrugged, 'I've seen them drifting in and out of the trees.'

'You have?' she asked, surprised. 'I don't get it?'

'Maybe you have to be in a particular state of mind. You know, in the hospital, you were pretty upset. Maybe that's what brought it on,' he suggested.

'Maybe.'

'Why are you so worried about it? Do you want to see more ghosts?'

'Yes,' she laughed.

'Really?' he asked, his face askew.

She nodded, 'Mum told me I was special. She said something big was going to happen to me, and I think maybe it's got something to do with ghosts.'

'Don't you think it's got something to do with your tattoo? And the fact that you can run super-fast?'

'I can?' she asked, not realising it herself.

'You didn't realise?'

'Not really,' she said, shaking her head.

Jack threw his head backwards and let out a deep laugh, 'Oh Daisy... you make me laugh. You can run faster than anyone I've ever seen in my entire, short, life. You can sing like, like, well, like an angel and you have this weird tattoo that just appeared on your back. You ARE special in more ways than one. Did you never realise any of this?'

Daisy tried to make sense of what he was saying.

'You really think I can sing? And run fast?' she asked, and he laughed again.

'Yes... seriously! And, you're not going to like what I'm going to say, but your dad is the one person who can tell you the truth.'

'Bah,' she said, turning to look away from him as she crouched down and rubbed the dirt from a headless angel statue. 'Let's not talk about my dad.'

Jack raised his eyebrows, 'You might not want to talk about him, but he's the only one who can answer your questions, Daisy.'

She sighed, 'I know, Jack, I know.'

'Okay, so you're not ready to go and find him yet. But you will be at some point.'

She turned and stuck out her tongue before smiling, 'yeah, I know.'

'Come on, let's sit and sing something,' he suggested, holding out his hand as if she could hold it. She responded by holding out her own, and they pretended to hold each other's hands with a smile as he led her to the sleeping lion where they sat beneath it. There they opened their mouths and began to sing the Coldplay song that suited Daisy, the song she had been singing the first time he had ever heard that exquisite voice of hers.

'Para-para-paradise, Para-para-paradise, Para-para-paradise...'

Daisy was so captivated by the moment that she didn't even notice several dog walkers had stopped to listen. A middle-aged man and two young women all stood, entranced by the girl's beautiful voice. They didn't hear Jack's, of course. All they saw was a teenage girl with a mass of red hair, sitting beneath a lion singing a song. But it was almost as if they were in a trance, brought on by her voice. When the song finally came to an end, the three of them just stood watching her. Soon snapping out of it, they all clapped loudly, making Daisy open her eyes suddenly and jump upwards in shock.

'Wow, that was amazing,' said one of the two girls as she turned to go.

'You really ought to sign up for the X factor,' said the other, 'You'd surely win with a voice like that,' she smiled before walking away.

The man just smiled at her, tipped his hat and walked on. All three dogs glad to finally be able to continue their morning walks.

ﷺ   IO   ﷺ

It was Christmas day, and it was snowing. Bizarrely though, Daisy didn't feel the cold.

Jack had discovered a secret place in the cemetery for them to sleep, an area protected from the elements and strangers that wandered through the park.

The catacombs beneath the War Memorial weren't creepy, not to her or Jack anyway. It was like her new home. She felt incredibly safe down there, especially with Jack, to keep her company.

He'd found it by following a ghost who wandered down there one day. Although the main entrance to the catacombs had been closed up, the spirit had led him to a secret passageway. The moment he'd entered it, he'd known that Daisy would love it down there. She'd feel safe, and that was all that mattered to him now.

Daisy had collected several old candles that she'd found in the back of the old corner shop. Shariq had let her keep them, so she'd taken them back to the catacombs, where she'd kept them for a special occasion. One like today, she thought.

Lighting them, Daisy then opened the bag that Balvinder had given her and took out the food that had been so carefully prepared by the older woman.

Aromas of spices filled the room, and Daisy smiled as she began to tuck in.

'I wish you could taste this, Jack,' she said as he just sat and watched her eat with a smile on his face.

'Yeah, I know. I do miss it, food, that is.'

'I'm sorry, Jack.'

'What for?'

'It's Christmas Day, and you're stuck down here with me. Don't you want to leave? You must miss your parents?'

'Of course, I miss them but... I'll have an eternity with them when I cross over. I don't want to, not yet anyway.'

'Would you know what to do when the time comes? I mean, is there a light or something?' she asked.

Jack turned to look over his shoulder with a smile, 'Yeah, it's there, always there right behind me.'

'Sometimes I wish I could cross over with you,' she admitted without even thinking about it.

'No, Daisy,' he scolded. 'Don't you dare think like that.'

Daisy looked up at him suddenly, her face reddening.

'You have your whole life to look forward to. Don't even think about dying yet. It's not your time.'

'Sorry,' she whispered.

'It's okay,' he whispered back before he glided upwards with a giggle as he suddenly started to sing,

'Jingle Bells, Jingle Bells, Jingle all the way.... oh what fun....'

Daisy began to giggle before she started to sing along with him.

Soon, they could hear another voice. At first, Daisy was so startled that she quietened into silence, but the sound was so jolly and fun that she carried on.

And then, another voice joined in and another and another until it sounded like a full choir singing Christmas Carols.

As the song came to an end, Daisy laughed as the other voices cheered, but not one showed themselves to her. So she began to sing another.

'On the Twelfth Day of Christmas, my true love sent to me.....'

The voices sang with her, full of joy and excitement, like they hadn't sung in a long time.

As they sang the last few words, Daisy stopped singing and just listened, hoping that at least one of the ghosts might reveal themselves to her.

And sure enough, one by one, she watched in delight as their forms began to materialise in front of her. Soon, about twelve ghosts sat quietly in a circle, all grinning from ear to ear.

'Hello dear,' said a lady of about 40 with curly blonde hair pinned up in true 1920s style. She wore a beautiful pleated blue dress and blue shoes. A trickle of dried blood stuck to the side of her face.

'H..hi,' replied Daisy.

'We've been watching you, you know?'

'Why... why did you wait so long to show yourselves?'

The lady smiled, 'we didn't want to frighten you,' she answered.

'Oh... okay. What's your name?'

'I'm Elizabeth. It's a pleasure to meet you, Daisy,' she smiled.

'It's nice to meet you too.'

The other ghosts introduced themselves. They included a man called Simon, who was about 30. He wore seventies-style clothes and had a huge afro. He also had a hole in his chest.

Terence was around 60, his cheeky face was deathly pale, and he was missing an arm as well as his left ear. Charlotte was the youngest of the group. She looked like a regular girl of about 18 or so and had long wiry auburn hair that draped down to her bottom. Daisy had never seen anyone so thin. Her face was gaunt and pale, and her expression looked like she was going to sick. But she was friendly, like all of them were.

'We've never had anyone sing Christmas carols here before,' she whispered. 'It's nice. It brings back memories of when I was alive,' she sighed.

Daisy was desperate to know how these people died, but she knew to ask the question this soon after meeting them might scare them off. It might be a bit, you know, personal.

For some time, they sat chatting about Christmases gone by, in between a good old sing-song, but later on, there seemed to be a heaviness in the air. There was no reason for it. It just changed the ambience in the catacombs. A slight breeze blew out the candles, and when Daisy went to re-light them, she noticed that everyone, except Jack, had vanished.

'What happened?' she whispered a bit freaked out. 'Where did they go?'

Jack shrugged his shoulders but shivered at the same time.

'What was that?' she asked.

Jack's expression suddenly changed, and the smiley boy she knew disappeared.

Daisy felt a shift in temperature and the hairs on the back of her neck prickled. Shivering, she climbed back into her sleeping bag and zipped it up tightly.

'Jack?' she whispered. 'Jack... where are you?'

When he didn't return or respond, Daisy pulled the cover over her head and closed her eyes.

Jack didn't come back for three days. When he did eventually show himself, something about him had changed. Daisy noticed it immediately.

'Jack? Where the hell did you go? I've been worried sick,' she scolded as she watched him float around the sleeping lion before he settled down in front of her.

'Well?'

'Well, what?'

'Where have you been?'

'I... I don't know.'

'What do you mean you don't know?'

'I mean exactly that... I don't know where I've been. The last thing I remember was singing Christmas carols with you in the catacombs. Why? I haven't been gone long, have I?' he asked.

'Long? You were away for three days,' she almost shrieked angrily.

Jack looked shocked.

'But... but, it seemed like I was just there with you.'

'Yeah well, you weren't. You left me alone, for three whole days.'

Jack lifted his face to look into her eyes, stroking his hand on her cheek. 'I... I'm sorry, Daisy. I don't know what happened.'

A tear fell down her cheek as she realised something freaky was going on, and whatever it was, she was determined to get to the bottom of it.

'It's okay, Jack. I'm sorry for freaking out. It wasn't your fault.'

'So you have absolutely no memory since the catacombs?'

Jack shook his head silently.

'What about the others?'

'What others?'

'The ghosts.'

'What ghosts?'

'You know, Elizabeth, Terence, Charlotte, Simon and the others,' she replied.

Jack laughed, 'I have no idea what you're talking about, Daisy. I've not met any ghosts around here. You know that.'

Daisy squinted at him, 'Jack, they introduced themselves to us the other day, and they sang carols with us. Don't you remember?'

Again he laughed, 'You're so funny, Daisy. There was nobody with us. It was just you and me, the candles and the songs.'

But Daisy shook her head firmly, 'No Jack, you're wrong. What's happened to you?'

Jack gulped, suddenly realising that something had indeed happened to him. His memory had all but disappeared.

'I'm surprised you even know me,' she huffed.

'Of course, I know you!'

'How did we meet?' she asked.

'That day in the park... you were, um... you were...'

Daisy raised her eyebrows.

'Drawing?'

'Um, yeah, I guess you were drawing.'

'What happened to your house, Jack?'

'My house? What house?'

'The house where you grew up? The house you lived with your parents?'

'I don't know what you're talking about. There's no house,' he chuckled nervously.

'Jack... how did you die?' she whispered.

'Die?' he asked, a silly grin across his face, 'now I know you're messing with me. I didn't die,' he laughed as he rolled back, so he lay on the ground across from her.

Daisy's eyes opened wide. Jack had forgotten almost everything about his life. The only thing he did know was her.

{ 12 }

The next few days were tough. After Daisy tried to explain to Jack what had happened, he'd gotten angry and disappeared again.

She'd told him about his mum and dad and the house fire, and she'd even ventured out of the park to show him the charred remains of their semi-detached house, where he had lived all 17 years of his life. But he had no idea. He acted as if he'd never seen the place before and after a few more hours of Daisy trying to drum it into his head, he'd shouted at her to shut up and had walked away.

She had no idea where he was, what he was doing, or if he was even okay. Can a ghost feel pain, she thought? She certainly hoped not.

After his first disappearance, she was beginning to get used to being alone again. She blocked him and her parents out of her mind and thought of nothing but survival and how she was even surviving in the first place.

She'd noticed things within her were changing. She barely felt the cold, she could go days without drinking much water at all, and when running, she realised she was fast, like superhuman fast. And then, in her burgeoning anger at Jack, she'd kicked a tree, knocking it entirely to the ground, realising that she also had, like superhuman strength.

What was going on? Did it have something to do with the tattoo? Perhaps now she was on her own, she should track down her dad and find out the truth once and for all.

But once she'd made up her mind that she needed to do just that, something happened.

Every evening before she called it a night, Daisy would walk around the grounds of Abney park and enjoy the peacefulness and the solitude in the dim light of dusk. But that night proved to be quite different.

She could feel it in the air, the sensation that she wasn't alone in the cemetery. And it wasn't the ghosts or the animals in the undergrowth. This was different. Her senses on full alert, Daisy was cautious about making little noise as she walked slowly and carefully through the gravestones, past the sleeping lion and beyond the numerous headless statues of angels scattered among the trees.

When she heard a howl, she stopped dead in her tracks and listened intently, her eyes skimming the area all around. The sound was followed by laughter, and not the fun kind. Immediately she knew that she was dealing with a group. Her first instinct was to run but, not knowing which direction they were coming from, she climbed the nearest tree. Seconds later, she sat on a stout branch, barely breathing. She'd never even realised she was capable of climbing trees and to do so at such speed shocked her. But she didn't have time to think about that. She knew those people in the park were bad news, and she didn't want them to catch her.

Silently waiting, she barely took a breath as she watched the group grow nearer.

There were four men, three women and two incredibly large dogs. As they approached, Daisy bit her lip. They weren't dogs. They were wolves and were on to her scent, sniffing all around the area. Fortunately, they seemed to lose interest, and neither of them looked upwards.

A pretty girl with long blonde dread-locked hair walked by the side of one of the animals, occasionally stroking the soft black fur on its back lovingly.

The other woman draped herself across a guy who wore black from head to toe. His shoulder-length black hair framed his handsome, yet pale and gaunt face. It was clear that they all looked up to him. Suddenly, the other beast howled loudly. Daisy watched in horror as his fur seemed to loosen and break apart. She heard its bones seem to crack beneath its skin and with her eyes wide open in terror, the wolf's limbs lengthened, its jaw pulled inwards until standing beneath the tree where she hid, stood a naked man.

She placed her hand over her mouth to stop the scream that threatened to pierce the night sky. She gulped back the tears and shook her head. A werewolf? Were they real? Her imagination went wild as she began to realise her world would never be the same again.

'Get him some clothes,' said their leader to the girl with the dreadlocks. She smiled, temporarily appreciating the naked form that stood in front of her. He grinned back at her, and she licked her lips before turning away and delving into the large holdall one of the others had carried.

She handed him a pair of black jeans, black boots and a black t-shirt.

Daisy watched as he slowly dressed. As much as she was terrified, curiosity took over. Apart from on TV, she'd never seen a naked man before.

Once dressed, she noticed the other wolf continued to walk circles around the group, occasionally walking a little further away to sniff the perimeter. He was clearly keeping watch.

Daisy's eyes grew tired as she rested her head against the tree trunk. But she forced herself to keep them open. She refused to fall asleep. Not while this strange group remained underfoot.

'Drake,' said the brunette. 'We have company,' she snarled with a smile.

Shocked and scared half to death, Daisy caught her breath. Had they spotted her?

But it wasn't her they were referring to. Someone had drifted into their circle. Almost like he was under a spell. Jack.

Daisy held her breath as she watched him hover in between them.

'Jack,' she mouthed silently.

'Well, what do we have here?' said the man called Drake.

'Its the boy again. I touched him a few days ago,' said the

brunette, who now stood with her hands on her hips. She licked her lips and held out her hand towards the spirit.

As her hand found his centre, Jack seemed to convulse.

But he was a ghost, how could he be affected, thought Daisy.

She wanted to help but knew there was nothing she could do. These were dangerous people. At least Jack was already dead, she thought guiltily.

Instead, she just sat motionless and helpless, watching from above as Jack was pulled and prodded by the young woman.

'Hello Jack,' she said to him. 'Its good to see you again.'

Jack hovered, his feet barely touching the ground with his head drooped forward.

'Well, aren't you going to say hello?' she asked as she prodded him again, causing his head to flick upwards.

'H...h...hello,' he whispered.

'Hello, what?' she probed.

'H..ello Bea...trice.'

The woman laughed and clapped her hands together. 'Aw, you remembered. How sweet. Now tell me, what have you been up to?'

Jack said nothing.

'What's the matter, don't you remember?' said the girl with dread-locked hair, laughing. She was sitting on the ground with her arm around the man who'd earlier transformed from a wolf.

'Come on, Jack, I only played with parts of your memory. Tell me what you've done since you last saw me?'

Jack looked up at her and opened his mouth, 'I...I... went to see Daisy. She, she told me I was dead,' he stuttered.

Daisy held her breath.

'Daisy? Who is this Daisy?'

Oh no, please don't tell them about me, thought Daisy.

'Daisy's my girl. She lives in the park.'

Momentarily forgetting about everything that surrounded her, Daisy's heart did a little jump. He called me his girl.

'She lives in the park? What? Do you mean this park? Abney Park?'

Jack nodded, and Daisy was brought back to reality with a bang.

'Well, well, well... looks like we've got a runaway in our midst,' said Drake.

'She sounds like fun, Drake,' said the dread-locked girl, 'can we find her? Can we play with her?'

Drake knocked his head backwards and laughed with his eyes closed.

'If you need another plaything to keep you occupied Darcey, sure.'

Oh My God, they're going to kill me.

$\maltese$ 13 $\maltese$

ortunately for Daisy, the group hadn't found her, and they hadn't killed her. Not yet, anyway. She'd stayed up there in that sturdy tree all night and just before dawn they'd finally gathered their things and left the park. Jack had been allowed to leave hours before, but Daisy had no idea where he'd gone.

When she knew it was safe, she expertly climbed down the tree and rushed to her hiding place inside the catacombs. Snuggling down into the sleeping bag, she closed her eyes and slept for as long as she could. Well, for as long as the nightmares would allow anyway.

Giant wolves chased her through the forest until she reached the tunnels beneath ground, escaping just moments before their deadly sharp claws tore at her skin. Breathing deeply, Daisy scurried through the darkness, but she wasn't alone. She could feel their breath on her skin, ghosts followed her. At every move, another one appeared until there were so many underground with her that she couldn't breathe. Her lungs felt tight, and she spluttered, gagging for breath, wheezing and coughing until she awoke with a start, covered in a light film of sweat.

Moments later, when she realised she was safe, Daisy laid back down and breathed in and out, in and out, calming her breath until it was finally back to normal.

It was just a dream, she thought, just a terrible dream.

'Daisy?' said a woman's voice out of nowhere.

'Ah,' she gasped.

'Oh, sorry,' said Charlotte, one of the ghosts from the other night who appeared in front of her. 'I didn't mean to startle you.'

'That's okay,' muttered Daisy self-consciously pulling the cover up to her ears.

'I, erm, I saw Jack earlier, and he seemed, well, weird. He didn't remember me.'

'Yeah I know, his memory has gone all weird... it's because of that scary woman.'

'What scary woman?' asked Charlotte.

'From that gang that was in the park earlier.'

'Oh yeah, I've seen them here before. I always keep my distance.'

'That's wise... I watched what they did to Jack. It wasn't pleasant.'

'Wh...what did they do to him?'

'I dunno, it was weird. She put her hand right into him. I could see he was uncomfortable. She said something about his memory being lost, and she made him tell her about me. I think they want to, well, I think they want to k...kill me.'

Charlotte gasped.

'How can they do that to a ghost?' she asked, afraid.

'I wish I knew. But I do know that they are evil and they're different. Two of them are...were...'

'What, Daisy, what?'

She gulped loudly before continuing, 'Werewolves. Two of them are werewolves, Charlotte. I saw one of them change. It was terrifying.'

'What are you going to do?'

'Me?' replied Daisy, 'I... don't know.'

'Maybe you should get out of Abney Park. Maybe you should run away, go somewhere safe,' she suggested as she floated around the catacombs.

'But I feel safe here. This is my home.'

'It is? But, but you must have a proper home somewhere?'

Daisy sighed and sat up straight.

'I did but not any more. This is my home now.'

'I miss my home, and I miss my Mum and Dad. If I had the chance to go back, I would take it like a shot.'

'How long have you... have you...'

'What? Been dead?' Charlotte interrupted, and Daisy nodded.

'A while, I guess. You lose all track of time when you're like this. I dunno, what year is it?'

'2012.'

'Really?' she said, shocked. 'I died in 1994.'

'How?' whispered Daisy.

Charlotte turned from her and floated away for a moment. Then she stopped and turned back, and before Daisy knew it, the girl was sitting beside her.

'Liver failure caused by bulimia... I was stupid. I was so desperate to be thin that I couldn't see myself the way I really was. I made myself so sick day after day after day. In the end, my body couldn't take it any more, and I died in the hospital. I can't bear... the....p...p...pain I caused my family. I hate myself for that,' she said, trying to punch herself in the stomach.

'I'm so sorry,' whispered Daisy.

'Don't be. It was my fault. Completely and utterly, my fault.'

'But why are you still here? Why didn't you, you know, cross over?'

Charlotte shrugged, her knees up to her chin. 'I just wasn't ready to, I guess. I felt too guilty to leave my parents. I dunno,' she shrugged again.

'Why don't you cross over now?'

'I haven't seen the light for a long time. I wouldn't know how,' she said sadly.

'You mean you're stuck here?'

Charlotte nodded, 'I guess.'

'Is there anything I can do to help?'

The smile almost lit up Charlotte's gaunt face, 'I wish you could, but I just don't know how.'

'Have you been to see your parents since, you know?'

'Since I died, you mean?'

Daisy nodded.

'I tried to, but I couldn't seem to leave the park.'

'That's weird. Have you tried to leave since?'

Charlotte shook her head.

'Come on, let's try now.'

'Really?'

'Yeah, come on,' yelled Daisy who was already at the secret entrance to the catacombs.

Peering out to make sure nobody was around, she rushed out and then covered up the entrance with twigs, branches and leaves. By the time she'd reached the old chapel, Charlotte was floating alongside her.

Daisy smiled when they reached the gate.

'Are you ready?' she whispered.

Charlotte looked terrified, but she nodded.

Walking through, Daisy turned around on the other side and waited for her new friend to try and make it through. The second she tried to float through, it was like she'd had an electric shock and she was dragged backwards, as if sucked into a vacuum, pulling her further back into the park.

'Daisy!' she yelled.

Dashing back into Abney Park, Daisy followed the young ghost until they both came to a halt outside the old chapel.

'Are you... are you... okay?' asked Daisy in shock.

'I... I think so,' she replied in horror.

'That was horrible. Did it hurt?'

But Charlotte shook her head, 'no, it just felt horrible. It was scary.'

'I wonder what's causing it. I mean, surely you weren't buried here were you? Is your grave in the cemetery?'

Charlotte shook her head, 'no, but I did ask my parents to scatter my ashes here, though.'

'Really? Well, maybe that's got something to do with it. Maybe you're trapped here because of that. Do you know if any of the other spirits are trapped too?'

Charlotte nodded, 'some of them are, yes.'

Daisy paced up and down the pathway, thinking about the ghosts.

'Maybe you have some unfinished business... and maybe you can't leave here until you've sorted it out?' she suggested.

'But don't you think that's a bit of a cliché?'

Daisy smiled, 'definitely, but what if it works? It could free you, Charlotte. It could help you to cross over.'

Charlotte's face slowly blossomed, and she beamed at Daisy who grinned back.

'I'll help you... I'll help you cross over.'

Daisy soon put the terror of the day to the back of her mind, and she began to feel good again. A feeling she hadn't had for such a long time. It was an emotion that felt right, a sentiment that made her realise this was what she was meant to do. She was meant to help these ghosts.

❄ 14 ❄

Stretching and yawning loudly, Daisy sat beside one of the headless angels with a piece of paper and pencil in her hand. Charlotte had given her as much information as she could remember. Her old address, her mum and dad's names, basically anything she thought might help Daisy to get to the truth about why she hadn't crossed over.

'Have you ever been touched by that woman, Charlotte?' she asked all of a sudden.

'Huh?' Charlotte responded with a confused look on her face.

'You know... the woman with the short brown hair, her from that scary gang.'

'Oh her, um, I don't think so. Why?'

'I was just wondering, making sure you haven't lost any important memories that's all.'

'I don't think so, but then would I remember if I had?'

Daisy shrugged, 'I guess you have a point. Look, I'm going to try and find your old house and see if I can talk to your parents. God knows what I'm going to say to them, though. They'll probably think I'm some psycho or something,' she laughed nervously.

Charlotte smiled sadly, 'I wish I could go with you.'

'I know.'

'Right, I may as well go now,' she said as she stood up and brushed the loose dirt from her jeans.

'Daisy?'

'Yeah?'

'When you talk to them... if they don't believe you... mention Brunhilda Van Horn. I think that might convince them that you're for real.'

'Brunhilda Van Horn? Who is that?'

Charlotte looked embarrassed as she faded away without another word.

'Okay, then... I'll go then, on my own. Bye,' she said more to herself than to anyone else.

She scribbled the name down on the piece of paper before folding it carefully and putting it in her back pocket. The pencil she placed in the front pocket of her coat and headed out of the park, remembering Charlotte's directions to the house she lived in before she died.

Strolling along the road, she felt like someone was watching her , so she stopped and turned around. Alone, except for a man walking his dog on the other side of the road, Daisy turned back and continued. But the sensation continued with her, and so she sped up a little. Rounding a corner, she came to a standstill, waited for a second before leaning round to have another look. Although she could see no-one, a familiar feeling overcame her, and she smiled.

'Hi Jack,' she said quietly.

Sure enough, Jack's ghost materialised in front of her.

'How did you know I was here?' he asked seriously.

She just shrugged and carried on walking.

'You seem annoyed,' he quite rightly deducted.

She said nothing.

'Have I done something to make you angry?'

She turned abruptly, and he stopped. Pointing her finger at him, she was about to speak when a jogger ran past looking at her oddly.

Daisy stopped, turned around and continued walking.

'Daisy, what's wrong?' Jack asked again.

Whispering out of the corner of her mouth, she said, 'You... you... told that vicious creepy gang about me, Jack. And now, I'm pretty sure they want to hurt me, or worse.'

Confusion filled his face, 'What gang? What are you talking about?'

'That gang with those... those... werewolves.'

Jack shook his head and started to laugh.

'You're such a joker, Daisy,' but when he saw her face, he stopped. 'You're n...n...not joking?'

She shook her head as they stopped at the traffic lights.

Sighing heavily, Daisy suddenly realised that he probably couldn't remember because she's screwed with his memory. He probably couldn't even remember their falling out either.

'Are you still insisting that you're not dead?' she asked.

Jack's expression answered her question, and she shook her head looking up at the grey sky.

'Oh boy,' she whispered. 'Look, Jack, I've got something really important to do just now. Let's talk about this later.'

'Can't I come with you?'

Looking at him as they crossed the road, 'whatever,' she said.

As they approached St. Elmo's Street, Daisy took her notes from her pocket, checked the house number and pushed it back in.

'Number 21,' she whispered under her breath.

'It's just here,' pointed out Jack as she stood outside the grandest house on the street.

Taking a deep breath, Daisy pushed open the gate and walked down the pathway until she reached the front door. She hoped they were in, as she noticed there was no car in the driveway.

Knocking, she waited a few moments. She could hear someone walking inside.

After a moment, Daisy stood looking at a frail woman in her 60s with long white hair tied up in a bun as she gingerly opened the door.

'Yes?' she asked.

'Mrs Freiling?'

'Yes.'

'I'm... I'm a friend of Charlotte's.'

Mrs Freiling took a step back, and with an intake of breath, her expression changed completely. 'I'm afraid that's not possible. You weren't even born when Charlotte, when Charlotte, well, you weren't even born...'

Daisy gulped. She knew this wasn't going to be easy.

'Um, I know Mrs Freiling. I, um, I've seen Charlotte recently.'

The woman closed her eyes and shook her head angrily.

'What are you playing at? My daughter died nearly 20 years ago,' and with that, she closed the door before Daisy had the chance to say another word.

'Great,' she mumbled, 'now what?'

'Speak to her through the letterbox,' suggested Jack.

Realising it was probably the only way, Daisy took out her notes once again and pushed open the letterbox.

'Mrs Freiling, please will you talk to me?'

The woman said nothing.

'Charlotte told me to mention Brunhilda Van Horn, Mrs Freiling...'

She heard the woman sob as she rushed away from the front door.

'Great, that didn't even work,' she whispered to herself before holding the letterbox open once more, 'Mrs Freiling, you can find me at Abney Park cemetery. I'm there every day. Please think about it. I need to talk to you.'

She waited for fifteen minutes, sitting quietly on the doorstep, but when there was no movement from inside, Daisy gave up.

'Come on, Jack. Let's go.'

15

'She wouldn't talk to me,' Daisy said as they arrived back at the park. Charlotte had been sitting patiently at the entrance. The moment she spotted Daisy and Jack, she jumped up eagerly awaiting news.

'No,' she sulked. 'Why not... did you mention Brunhilda?'

Daisy nodded sadly as the three of them began walking back through the trees, all with their heads hanging down.

Suddenly a whole host of ghosts appeared in front of them, making Daisy jump in surprise. Some she recognised, some she didn't.

'Well?' said a middle-aged lady with spiky red hair.

But Charlotte merely shook her head as all the ghosts sighed.

'I told you so... I told you some teenage girl wouldn't be able to help us.'

'Wh... what?' Daisy cried out, 'What do you mean?'

Charlotte turned to her new friend and answered for them. 'I told them about you, Daisy. I told them how you were going to help me cross over. They were hoping you could help them too.'

Daisy noticed the 'were'.

'Hang on a minute... give me a chance. Charlotte's mother wouldn't speak to me, that doesn't mean this won't work...'

Before she could say another word, they'd all vanished.

Throwing her hands up in the air, Daisy cursed under her breath. But a voice behind her startled her.

'Hello?'

Turning rapidly on the spot, Daisy could barely believe her eyes. It was Charlotte's mother.

'Mrs Freiling, you came.'

The woman was wrapped up in a warm winter coat, scarf, gloves and hat, but she still shivered.

'Shall we walk?' asked Daisy, thinking perhaps they could take shelter from the wind in the old chapel.

Mrs Freiling nodded, and the two began to stroll along the well-worn pathway.

'How did you know about... about Brunhilda Van Horn?'

'Charlotte told me.'

The woman held her face upwards towards the sky, closed her eyes for a moment and pursed her lips.

'Nobody knew about Brunhilda except for Charlotte and me. I've never told a soul,' she whispered.

Feeling someone else walking next to her, Daisy turned to see Charlotte smiling, looking across at her mother.

'She looks old,' she said, 'and sad... and so frail.'

Mrs Freiling stopped, turning to face Daisy, 'how do I know you're not just a scam artist? Tell me truly. How did you hear that name?'

Daisy's face screamed honesty as she said, 'As I said before, Charlotte told me.'

'Tell her it's the name we gave to my special friend,' said Charlotte.

'Charlotte's telling me to tell you that Brunhilda Van Horn is the name you gave to her special friend.'

The woman's hands covered her mouth, 'she's here?'

Daisy nodded.

'Special friend?' whispered Daisy to Charlotte, who looked away embarrassed before whispering, 'she was my childhood imaginary friend.'

Daisy smiled, 'she's telling me she was her imaginary friend when she was a child.'

'Oh My God, Charlotte... can you hear me, my princess?'

Charlotte stood in front of her mother with such a wide smile. 'It's been a long time since I heard her call me her princess.'

'She can hear you. She's standing in front of you. She said it has been a long time since anyone called her that.'

Tears flowed freely down the woman's face.

'Mrs Freiling, Charlotte has been trapped here all these years. I'm trying to help her cross over, but something is stopping her from doing so. We hoped that you might be able to help her?'

'She's been trapped here? Oh My Goodness. My poor princess. If only I'd known. Charlotte I'm so sorry.'

'Can you ask her about daddy?'

Daisy nodded, 'She wants to know about her dad.'

Mrs Freiling looked up in surprise, 'Jim? She doesn't know? Jim died last year of a heart attack,' she sobbed, 'I'd hoped the two of you would be together by now.'

Charlotte looked like she'd been kicked in the stomach. 'Daddy's' dead?' She cried, 'Oh no... Daddy.'

'We scattered his ashes here too, in the hope that you'd be together forever.'

'I'm so sorry, Mrs Freiling,' said Daisy as she watched mother and daughter sobbing together but so far apart.

'What about Daphne?' asked Charlotte.

'Your daughter wants to know about Daphne.'

Mrs Freiling's tears slowly dried up as she smiled, 'Daphne is doing so well. She got a degree in food and nutrition. She married a doctor. They have two daughters, Charlotte and Angelica.'

Charlotte's eyes widened in amazement, 'My little sister!' she exclaimed.

'She's delighted,' Daisy whispered as she placed her hand on Mrs Freiling's arm.

As Charlotte smiled at the wonderful news, her face began to change - the gauntness and translucence disappeared altogether. She looked healthy for the first time in 20 years.

'Charlotte,' said Daisy, 'you look so different. You look healthy.'

'I feel good too... oh,' she said.

'What? What is it?' asked Daisy.

'What's happening? asked Mrs Freiling, who wished she could see her daughter for the last time.

Charlotte smiled, 'there's a light that's getting brighter. It's pink and blue and sparkly. I have such an overwhelming sense of peace, Daisy. Oh,' she suddenly sobbed, 'Daddy!'

'I think she's ready to go, Mrs Freiling. She sees your husband.'

The woman shook her head in disbelief as tears of joy and sadness poured from her eyes.

'Goodbye, my princess. It won't be long until I'm with you,' she whispered as Charlotte began to walk away. But just before she disappeared she turned back with a beautiful smile, 'tell Mum I love her so much and thank you, Daisy. Thank you so very much. I'll never forget you,' and then she was gone.

'She's gone,' whispered Daisy, 'She wanted you to know how much she loves you.'

Mrs Freiling nodded, 'I know... I know,' she said as she dabbed at her cheeks with a handkerchief. 'I don't even know your name?'

'It's Daisy.'

'Thank you so much, Daisy. I guess Charlotte just needed to know what had happened to us all and she would never have been able to find out were it not for you. So thank you, thank you so very much,' she said as she turned and walked away, past the sleeping lion and the headless angels.

Daisy stood watching her go, a feeling of peace enveloping her as a few happy tears slowly rolled down her face.

16

One night while the moon was exceptionally bright, the sounds of howling chilled Daisy to the core. As it had been such a lovely night, Daisy had decided to sit near the big headless statue with her sketchbook. It had been such a long time since she'd done any drawings and there was just something about the unusually large moon sitting behind the statue that made her want to remember it and the best way to do that was to sketch it.

The drawing was just about complete when the howling started. The terror almost prevented her from moving, keeping her stuck to the same spot. 'Move, move, move,' she whispered to herself as the sounds got closer and closer until finally, the adrenaline pulsing through her body allowed for movement. But there wasn't enough time to get back to the catacombs. She had no choice, therefore, than to escape upwards.

Climbing the nearest tree, she'd just got high enough when she saw them. Holding her breath, Daisy watched as the first wolf sniffed at the spot where she had been sitting just moments before. He wandered around, smelling the ground, getting closer and closer to the tree where she found herself clinging to.

As the others arrived, the dread-locked woman's eyes appeared to be glowing yellow. Daisy gulped.

The second wolf followed behind her, then the awful memory

busting brunette and her man, the leader walked into the clearing last.

They were murmuring, laughing about having stolen some precious item. Daisy heard them mention something about a museum, but before she had the chance to listen to anything further, she spotted her pencil hanging out of her jacket pocket.

With eyes wide open in fear, Daisy realised she was unable to catch it in time as she clung to the tree. So she watched it fall like it was moving in slow motion, out of her pocket and was slowly carried on the breeze until it bounced onto the ground below.

How could such a small thing make such a loud noise, Daisy would never understand.

The moment it hit the ground, both wolves' ears pricked upwards, followed by their eyes. Daisy would never forget that moment.

The second they laid their eyes on her, the dread-locked girl looked up right at her as if they had communicated telepathically. Her eyes seemed to glow as she hissed with an evil smile spreading across her face.

'Well, well, well,' she said as the other two turned to see what all the fuss was about. 'What have we here? This must be the Daisy that Jack mentioned.'

Daisy didn't know what to do. She could climb down and try and outrun them, but she knew that would never work, even with her superhuman speed, would the wolves match it? Looking across at the nearby trees, she saw her only means of escape. She would have to jump from tree to tree until she could either get out of the park or into her secret hiding place. The trouble with that is that they might see her go in and she certainly didn't want that. She had no choice. She would have to try and escape from the park.

The wolves watched her every move while the three 'humans' goaded her, assuming she was just a regular runaway hiding in a tree.

Perhaps the element of surprise would slow them down a little.

She didn't want to wait and see what they would do. She just knew she had to escape

So she took a deep breath and threw herself onto the closest tree, grabbing it with all her strength like an Amazonian monkey. If only she had a long tail, she thought as she then went on to the next.

She could hear the 'humans' yelling at her, and the wolves were snarling, following her trail from beneath her.

'Get her!' shouted the leader as one of the wolves jumped as high as possible.

Fortunately for Daisy, it wasn't quite high enough, and as she grabbed hold of the next tree, she left the wolf behind slightly. However, the next tree wasn't as sturdy; it refused to hold her weight, and so she hung, clinging on, as it drooped, creaking, threatening to break directly above the gang.

A wolf snapped at her feet, grabbing her and pulling her down, tearing the skin on her ankle. She winced, and with as much of her strength as she could muster, she kicked it full force on the head, temporarily stunting it as it released her.

With a split second to spare, she grabbed hold of the nearest branch and flung herself on to it before eventually landing on to the gate's wall. Stopping briefly to catch her balance, she ran along the top of the wall, like a tightrope walker, all the time listening to check where the wolves were, snapping beneath her feet.

She could hear the cackle of the brunette's laugh as she enjoyed the thrill of the hunt, confident that she would have a plaything for later.

But Daisy had other ideas, and so, she turned and took one last look at the gang and catapulted herself out of the park, landing on her feet. She ran as fast as she possibly could until she reached Balvinder and Shariq's corner shop.

Tears fell down her cheeks, and the adrenaline continued to flow as she banged hard on the door.

'Please let me in Shariq... please,' she shouted, banging, banging, banging.

Finally, after a couple of minutes, she noticed the shop light switch on and Shariq hurried to open the door.

She pushed it open and slammed it shut behind her.

'Switch off the light, switch off the light,' she shouted.

Shariq did exactly as she said while trying to calm the young girl down.

'Are you hurt, Daisy? Are you injured? What happened? What

happened?' he said as Daisy burst into tears and leaned back against the wall, sliding down until she sat in a heap on the floor.

'I'm okay,' she said, 'I'm okay. Thank you, thank you,' she sobbed.

'Shariq... what on earth is going on down there?' shouted Balvinder from the top of the stairs.

'It's okay — no need to worry. We're coming up. Come on, Daisy, get up, get up. Come upstairs, and we'll fix you a nice cup of sweet tea. It's okay now. It's over. It's over...'

❧ 17 ☙

Daisy had refused to tell Balvinder and Shariq what had happened. They knew she was a homeless girl, but they also knew not to ask questions. Even though she knew they trusted her, she knew she couldn't tell them the truth. She had a feeling inside her that said nobody should know about her abilities or the fact that werewolves existed.

Slowly she began to accept that she was seriously different from most people and that she was strong enough to come to terms with it. She had managed to escape the gang. If she did it once, she could do it again. Nobody was going to frighten her away from her home.

Daisy spent the next few months in a frenzy of helping numerous ghosts to cross over. But at the same time, she tried to return the memories of those touched by the weird brunette in the scary gang.

Luckily, she had so far managed to evade capture, but she had seen them since in the park at night on several occasions. Some local ghosts had warned her when they were coming, giving her time to escape to her hiding place within the secret catacombs. She just hoped that none caught would give her 'home' away.

Jack was still with her, promising to stay by her side for the foreseeable future. But one morning, she knew it was finally time for him to go.

She'd found him wandering through the trees like a lost puppet on a string, not knowing which way to go. He'd been touched by her again, and enough was enough. Jack had been that woman's target too many times now, and his memories were beginning to confuse him.

'Jack, this can't go on any more. You must cross over and join your family.'

'I don't know what you mean?'

'Jack, surely by now, you must realise what you are? You died in that house fire months ago. You've only been staying here for me and I, I think it's time for you to go.'

Looking forlorn, Jack stared at the muddy ground, 'I... I know, I'm a ghost, aren't I?'

Daisy nodded, 'I've been telling you for months, but you never believe me. You usually go off in a huff. But it's time to face up to it, Jack. It's time for you to join your family.'

'But... but, who is my family, Daisy?'

'Your mum and dad, Jack. They're waiting for you.'

'But what if I don't recognise them?'

A smile crossed Daisy's face, 'I have a feeling that all your memories will return the moment you step into that light. You'll know them immediately.'

'But... but I don't want to leave you, Daisy. I can't leave you. I promised that I would never leave you.'

'That was when I'd lost everything, Jack. I was lost. But I'm not lost any more I've found myself here, helping all these trapped spirits. I feel like this is what I'm meant to do, at least it's part of what I'm meant to do.'

'What do you mean?'

Shrugging her shoulders, Daisy kicked the dirt absent-mindedly, 'I dunno. I feel like I'm meant to be a part of something big. I don't know what yet but I know that it's coming. I can't explain it except that I know I'm in the right place now and I'm okay. I'll be okay. I'm finally able to let you go, Jack.'

The expression on his face made her stomach feel like it was tied up in a massive knot and she felt so guilty, but she knew, deep down, that he wasn't meant to stay on this earth any longer.

'But, Daisy... I, I...'

'I know, Jack.'

Looking back to the floor, he suddenly rushed right up to her and shook his head determinedly.

'I'm not leaving until you've found your father,' he said, crossing his arms with a smirk.

She knew he meant it, and she also knew that he was right. It was time that she tracked him down. She was ready to be reunited.

Holding her hands up in submission, she smiled and shook her head, 'Okay, okay... I'll find my dad, and you cross over.'

'Not until you've found him though,' he winked as Daisy nodded with a sigh.

oOo

FINDING THE DRUNK HOMELESS MAN TURNED OUT TO BE A LOT easier than you'd imagine. With the help of quite a few ghosts, it was a piece of cake. She knew exactly where he was, and she was ready to fetch him.

Waiting for nightfall, Daisy knew that a petite teenage girl carrying a fully grown man through town and then to the cemetery might get some odd attention, especially if she planned on doing it at speed.

So after her shift at the corner shop, instead of heading home, she took a slow walk, a couple of miles to central Hackney. Once she'd arrived, she found a secluded spot to eat her dinner, kindly provided by Balvinder. Then she sat for hours waiting for the streets to clear in the darkness.

After midnight, she finally felt ready to go and see her father, and so she began the short walk to the spot where she'd been told he frequently beds down for the night, not too far from the end of Church Street.

Walking through the shopping district, Daisy couldn't help but look longingly in the shop windows. It was a long time since she'd had the money to be able to walk into a clothes shop and buy whatever took her fancy. Like every January, in the sales, her mum had always given her £100 spending money and told her to buy whatever she wanted. She stood for a moment with her hands on the glass, looking at the latest styles on the faceless mannequins.

Daisy sighed and looked down at the old pair of skinny jeans that were ripped at the ankle and were becoming more and more stained despite the weekly wash Balvinder gave them.

One day, she thought, one day, things will be different.

The sound of breaking glass interrupted her thoughts, and she turned quickly to see a couple of teenage boys laughing as they threw a second beer bottle at the wall.

She withdrew out of the street light and continued to walk silently in the shadows beyond, careful to avoid attention.

Daisy spotted a nearby police car come to a halt by the kerb. Two officers stepped out and approached the drunken boys, who were growing louder by the minute. Daisy waited for them to turn away from her before she rushed across the street and carried on walking until she reached the place she expected to find her father.

It was a short narrow alleyway with a dead end. Right at the back, she could see someone leaned against the wall with a bottle in his hand. The familiar smell of alcohol and stale body odour made her nose wrinkle in disgust.

'Dad?' she said as she tiptoed closer.

The man stopped, mid-drink, and slowly moved the bottle away from his lips.

'Dad?' she asked again, a little louder.

Trying to stand, she watched him sway uncontrollably. Rushing forward to catch him as he fell, Daisy felt a familiar tug in her chest. She'd missed him so much. And she'd only just realised.

'It's okay, Dad. I've got you. I'm going to take you somewhere safe. I'm going to look after you now, Dad,' she whispered as her eyes welled up.

$$\textbf{18}$$

Getting him 'home' had been surprisingly easy. Using her peculiar new-found strength, she hoisted him across her back and ran, keeping away from the street lights and stopping at the sight of anyone wandering the streets, casually leaning him against the wall. Once the person had passed, she'd hoist him right back up and continue running until arriving back at Abney Park in the early hours of the morning.

Getting him into the catacombs was a little more difficult considering the entrance was quite tight but she'd finally managed, soon falling asleep next to her snoring father in the darkness.

Waking up the following morning, she was startled to find her father had disappeared. Cursing under her breath, she'd rushed up into the crisp air, only to find him kneeling quietly inside the old chapel whispering.

'...very sorry. I shouldn't have left her like that but look at her. I knew she'd do better on her own,' he coughed before continuing, 'I'll never forgive myself for doing what I did, but I miss you. God, I miss you...' he sobbed, his whole body shuddering.

Daisy tiptoed back outside and sat down on an old rock covered in moss and dirt. Was he praying? Was he speaking to Mum? Could he see her, thought Daisy. No, I saw her cross over the day she died.

As she sat pondering, Beau appeared through the old doorway.

'Daisy?' he croaked, holding his head as if in pain.

'Dad? Are you okay?'

Wincing and nodding at the same time, Daisy was shocked to see him in daylight. His handsome face had dramatically changed since she'd last seen him. The alcohol abuse had taken its toll on his looks and his health. Dull, red ones replaced his once attractive clear green eyes with heavy lids and deep bags beneath them. His skin looked pale and grey, and his newly grown beard and long straggly hair were full of greying hairs.

'I need a drink,' he whispered, half smiling.

Daisy shook her head, 'No, Dad... that's enough. It's been long enough. It's time you pulled yourself together.'

'You don't understand, Daisy... I need it.'

Daisy stood her ground, 'You don't need it, Dad. It's making you ill.'

He rushed towards her and fell to his knees, 'I need it. I'm sorry, but I do, I need it. I need it.'

She watched as he begged her, his whole body shivering - not from the cold but his need for alcohol. Seeing him like that terrified her. She knew he needed medical help, but how could she offer him that?

'Okay,' she whispered. 'I'll help you but will you go back to the warmth and try to sleep. I'll see what I can do.'

After agreeing, she took him back to the catacombs, where she made him curl up in her sleeping bag. It didn't take long until he closed his eyes and was snoring again.

Content that he could be left alone for a while, Daisy decided to go for a walk through the park to clear her head, but before long she realised she wasn't alone. A ghost had appeared. One she hadn't seen before.

'Hello?' she asked the young man in the strange blue velvet jacket and trousers.

'Erm... hello?' he whispered nervously back.

'I'm Daisy.'

'Hello Daisy,' he answered shyly.

'Do you have a name?'

The man looked away from her and fiddled with the buttons on his jacket. 'I, erm. I don't know.'

'What do you mean, you don't know?'

'I...I... don't remember?'

Oh, not again, thought Daisy. That horrible woman had gotten to him too. As she looked at him, she realised he looked scared, alone and incredibly lost.

'That's okay. You're safe here with me. I have a perfect hiding place where you could stay for a while if you like, at least until you feel better. Until you remember who you are?'

The ghost looked around as if he was spooked and nodded.

She smiled and suggested he follow her.

'My dad is sleeping down there at the moment, but don't worry, you're completely safe with him. Everything is going to be okay, alright? I'll make sure of that,' she said warmly.

The ghost visibly relaxed as she showed him the way to the catacombs.

'It's well hidden,' she pointed. 'You're welcome to stay there as long as you need to, okay?'

He nodded and disappeared inside.

oOo

'JACK? YOU THERE?' SHE ASKED A LITTLE LATER AS SHE SAT beneath the sleeping lion, wondering what to do.

Jack appeared instantly with a smile.

'I take it you've been there the whole time?'

He nodded.

'What should I do? I don't know what to do?'

Jack approached her and placed his arm across her shoulders, making her smile.

'I wish I could feel that, Jack.'

'Me too.'

She looked at him and asked him again, 'What am I going to do? He looks so ill.'

'Can you take him to a hospital?'

'I don't know... will they even help him? Will they turn us away?'

'No... they wouldn't do that. I'm sure they'll do everything they can to help. I'll come with you if you like?'

Daisy smiled but shook her head, 'Jack,' she said, 'You made me a promise, remember?'

But he turned away from her with a sigh, 'but... but... you need me more now than ever before. You need me to help you with your dad.'

'No, Jack. Now I'm with my dad again; it's him and me. I have to help him on my own. He's my family, and it's time for you to be with yours. They're waiting for you.'

She thought she saw him wipe away a tear. Can ghosts cry?

'You know I'm right, Jack. You have to move on, just like me. I'll be happier knowing you are where you belong. You promised me, Jack.'

'I know,' he replied.

'Are you ready?'

Slowly, he looked deep into her eyes and nodded.

'I'm ready,' he croaked.

'I'm really going to miss you, Jack.'

'I'm really going to miss you too. I'll never forget you,' he whispered as he leaned forward and gently placed a kiss on her cheek. A kiss that she could have sworn she actually felt.

'I promise never to forget you too, Jack.'

'Daisy?' he asked.

'Yes?'

'I... I love you,' he whispered before he stood up and began to walk away.

'I love you too, Jack,' she said to him quietly. He turned to look at her with a smile and then before she knew it, he was gone.

Her stomach twisted and knotted and tears began to pour down her cheeks. But then she suddenly had the most overwhelming desire to sing, so she opened her mouth and very quietly began singing the song that had brought her and Jack together:

'Para-para-paradise, Para-para-paradise, Para-para-paradise ...'

❧ 19 ☙

Beau Madigan awoke with such intense aches and pains that he couldn't bear it. His body shook with such desperation and need for alcohol that he clambered out of the place Daisy called home and, without even telling her, he left Abney Park.

Daisy was busy elsewhere at the time, trying to convince a man in Highgate that his great, great, great, great grandfather was trying to communicate with him. The man was having none of it until Daisy's ghost mentioned he had buried treasure in the family garden, twenty-five yards due east from the ancient oak tree.

Then he had no trouble believing what she had to say. In fact, she went along with him, across the grounds of the grand old house and watched as he used an old spade to dig deep into the earth. When he hit upon something substantial, the ghost smiled at her and drifted away, immediately crossing through the bright light and over to the other side.

Daisy congratulated the man on his find and decided to leave.

She was worried about her dad and knew she needed to get back to check on him.

On her way back, she stopped in to see Balvinder and Shariq to ask their opinions on alcohol addiction. They both said her father should seek medical help, and so that's what she decided to do.

But on finding him gone on her return, Daisy sighed heavily and busied herself with helping another ghost to cross over.

She knew he'd come back. She didn't know how she knew; she just did.

Late that night, sure enough, she found him wandering around the gravestones of the cemetery, completely drunk with another bottle of vodka in his hands.

'Dad... again? You need to stop this. I wish you would stop it, for me. There's so much we need to talk about. I need you to tell me about the tattoo and why I'm so strong and fast and different. Please, Dad.'

Beau looked at her and dropped the bottle. It smashed against a gravestone just before he collapsed in a heap on the ground.

Daisy took a deep breath and sighed when a sudden noise in the darkness startled her. Worried it was that scary gang, her initial instinct was to disappear up a tree, leaving her father behind on the ground. She cursed to herself as she sat, watching her comatose father below. But it was too late to go and get him as a guy suddenly emerged through the trees.

She shivered, hoping it wasn't one of the members of that terrifying gang. He disappeared as quickly as he'd appeared so Daisy climbed back down to her father and scooped him up as fast as she could. She hid behind a massive tree for a moment and waited to see if the guy would return. Soon, he and eleven other teenagers reappeared. One of them even began to clear up the broken glass her father had broken.

Content that they were just regular teenagers, she stealthily disappeared again to another of her favourite spots: one of the largest headless angels in the park. Sitting down beneath it with her father by her side, Daisy thought of Jack. She smiled, remembering the times they had spent together. I hope he's happy with his mum and dad; she thought as that same sensation began to fill her belly again. The overwhelming desire to sing. Instead of the usual Paradise, she remembered a Lana Del Rey song that he'd liked called Born To Die:

'Feet don't fail me now...'

She was so wound up singing that song that she was completely unaware that someone had approached and suddenly a yelp pierced the air.

Daisy didn't even stop for breath, she grabbed her father and bolted back to the catacombs where she pushed her father inside, making sure he was still asleep, before venturing back into the trees, curious to find out what was going on.

Returning to the headless angel, she found the group had gone. She listened for sounds and could hear them inside the chapel. They're probably just here messing about, she figured so before she called it a night, she wandered over to the sleeping lion where she sat down for a moment and thought about the following morning when she planned on taking her father to the hospital.

Suddenly, the sound of breaking twigs made her jump, and she looked up to find two of the teenagers approaching her. She immediately jumped up, ready to bolt.

"Wait,' a pretty dark-haired girl all dressed in black said softly. 'Please, we're here to warn you. You're in danger. There are some evil, crazy guys coming for you. They'll be here really soon. You need to get away from here as quick as you possibly can or come with us, take my hand. We're going back to the chapel to the rest of our group. You'll be safe there...'

But the mere thought of being anywhere near that horrifying werewolf gang made Daisy run. She ran to the only place she knew she'd be completely safe.

Once inside the catacombs, curled up in a corner, Daisy began to have second thoughts. There was something about them, about that girl, that she felt a connection to, and it wasn't something she could explain. She just knew she had to go back.

Creeping back through the park, she managed to climb up into a tree overlooking the entrance to the old chapel, without any of the teenagers noticing. She just sat there, watching and listening.

'Please, we need to find him. You heard what the ghosts said. The evil ones would try and get to him. I don't even want to think about what they could do to him if they did,' said the dark-haired girl who'd tried to help Daisy before.

'He's a ghost, Em. What can they do to him that hasn't been done to him already?' asked a gorgeous girl with afro hair.

'You're joking, right? Did you see how terrified those other ghosts were of them? And what about poor Joe finding his way home, crossing over, where he belongs? I'm not giving up on him, Sis, and neither should you. It's not about the stupid task any more. It's about helping Joe. Our friend, Joe and I'm not leaving this place without him. If you all want to go, then go. I won't hold it against you. Nisha, please get the ghosts back so I can communicate with them before you go,' the dark-haired girl said.

'Hey, wait a minute. Nobody is leaving you,' said a cute tall guy who dragged her back towards him. 'I sure as hell am not going to. I'll stay until we've found him. I promise, okay?'

The others slowly began to step towards the girl, each placing a hand on her and nodding.

'I'm sorry, Sis. You're right. We're all in this together. Let's go and find him.'

Daisy seemed to have such a connection with them. She was so moved by what was happening that she felt the need to help, and she knew who they were talking about.

'You don't have to go anywhere,' she said.

She watched as they all dropped their hands from the girl and turned to face her.

'Daisy?' asked the girl.

Climbing down, she walked up to them and smiled sadly, nodding, 'How do you know me?'

'The ghosts told us your name. I'm glad you got away.'

Smiling nervously, Daisy replied, 'Only because of you. Thank you'.

'What did you mean, we don't have to go anywhere,' asked the other gorgeous girl.

'The ghost you're looking for, I know where he is. I've been keeping him safe for a couple of days. You called him Joe, right?' she asked.

The gorgeous girl nodded, 'That's his name, well Josiah. Josiah Grimshaw. He came with us from Andilyse Island last week, but he seems to have forgotten everything.'

'Can you take us to him?' asked the dark-haired girl.

Daisy nodded, 'Follow me,' she whispered as the group all began to trample after her, careful not to make too much noise.

'What is that?' asked the Indian boy who had appeared to her earlier as they approached the large memorial.

'It's a War Memorial,' said Daisy. 'There are catacombs beneath it. The main entrance has been blocked off, but I know a secret way in.'

'Cool,' said the first guy she'd seen as they walked around the memorial and then off to the side under a cluster of nearby trees. There was a hole in the ground with a tunnel that led towards the monument.

'He's hiding in there... with my Dad,' Daisy said shyly.

'Oh... okay. Nisha, over to you,' the dark-haired girl said with a smile.

'You want me to climb down there?' the Indian girl asked a little nervously.

'It's not as bad as it looks. It's quite clean actually, even though the entrance looks a bit dodgy,' said Daisy. 'Follow me.'

The Indian girl rubbed her chin and followed Daisy down into the tunnel. Daisy fidgeted around until a light was switched on.

'I always keep a few supplies down here,' she smiled as she held the torch upwards. 'Can you see Josiah?'

'No, he's not here.'

'Josiah?' she whispered.

'He doesn't remember his name, does he?'

'Oh yeah, I forgot about that. Hello, is there anybody here. Anybody ghostly? Can you show yourself?' asked the girl. 'Hello? We know you're here. We just want you to show yourself.'

Daisy's father mumbled something in his sleep before turning over and snoring, his sweatshirt lifted slightly, revealing his tattoo. The Indian girl gasped but said nothing. Instead, she turned to concentrate on Josiah.

'Look, we know who you are. We know you've lost your memory. We can help you. It's why we're here.'

'It is? You know who I am?' said a voice in the semi-darkness as a figure slowly started to emerge in the corner. The ghost of the young man sat huddled up, his face filled with confusion and fear.

'Your name is Josiah, Josiah Grimshaw. Does that mean anything to you?' asked the Indian girl as he shook his head. 'We're your friends. You came to London with two sisters, Lana Beth and

Emma Jane Morgan. Do you remember?' She asked. A faint flicker of familiarity crossed his eyes, and he sat up.

'Emma? It does seem familiar to me. Where is she?' he asked.

'She's above ground. We came here to find you. Will you return with us?' she asked.

He waited a moment before finally slowly nodding.

As they prepared to go, the dark-haired girl who appeared to be called Emma turned to Daisy.

'Daisy, will you come back with us?'

'Back where? And what about my Dad?'

'Emma? I saw her dad down there, and he's one of us. I saw the tattoo on his back. Which means Daisy is one of us too,' interrupted the Indian girl.

Daisy stopped herself from telling them about her tattoo. Although she felt connected to these people, she wasn't brave enough to show them, not yet anyway.

'I knew it,' said Emma, 'Look, Daisy, I can't explain exactly where we'll be going. Just know that you can trust us. And there are people there, people like you and me that would happily take you in. You can learn with us. I just know that you're meant to come back with us. There's this feeling in the pit of my stomach, and it's telling me that you should. Your dad can come, as well. He'll get the treatment he needs. I promise you; you won't regret it,' she said with her hands on Daisy's shoulders.

Just the thought that her father would get the treatment he needed was enough to make Daisy jump for joy. She would finally get her father back. She waited as the others stood slightly back, nodding.

'I have the feeling too,' said one.

'And me,' said two of the girls.

'I do too,' said the Indian boy before the rest of them all agreed.

Daisy's eye welled with tears as she looked around at the friendly faces staring at her hopefully. Finally feeling like she belonged, she nodded.

The group kept quiet, but their faces lit up, and they all grinned at her before giving each other high-fives. The first guy she'd seen offered to climb down into the catacombs to fetch her father, but she shook her head.

'There's really no need, thank you. I can do it myself.'

Within seconds, she had vanished before returning above ground carrying her father over her shoulder.

'Now that's what I'm talking about,' laughed the Indian boy, who turned his baseball cap backwards on his head as they began to exit the cemetery.

As they reached the main gates, Daisy turned back and took a long look at the place that had been her home for almost a year. She watched as a dozen or so ghosts appeared from nowhere to wave her off.

'Farewell, Daisy. Don't forget us, we're still hopeful you can help us,' said Elizabeth, one of the ghosts she'd met first.

'I won't Elizabeth. I'll be back to cross you all over. I promise. Bye,' she waved happily, knowing that she was finally going where she belonged.

oOo

If you enjoyed Daisy Madigan's Paradise, be sure to get your
copy of
The Ghost of Josiah Grimshaw,
the first full-length novel in The Praxos Academy series.
Read on for an excerpt...

20

EXCERPT: THE GHOST OF JOSIAH GRIMSHAW 1

Lightning shattered the darkness. Not even Emma's thick purple quilt could shut out the light as it filtered through to her closed eyelids. A low echo of rumbling thunder made its way across the North Sea towards Andilyse Island and she shivered. Suddenly something landed on top of her head and she shrieked. The sounds of laughter emanated from the bed across the room.

'Lana, you cow,' shouted Emma as she threw back the covers and tossed the pillow back at her sister who just shook her head and giggled.

'It's only a storm. There's nothing to be scared of.'

'There is everything to be scared of,' she replied as she cowered beneath the quilt again.

'Oh come on, Sis. We're quite safe here. This house has been standing for hundreds of years, it's not like it's going to collapse is it?'

'It nearly did the last time,' Emma croaked.

'That was like sixty years ago, Em, and none of the houses collapsed. The only thing that took the brunt of the storm was the pier.'

'And the church.'

'Exactly. None of the houses. Stop being such a coward. You're fifteen! It's a storm, it's rain, it's not the end of the world.'

'It was for all those poor people.'

'Oh stop being so dramatic. Things were different back in the 50s, Em. We're safe, now stop worrying.'

The sound of the front door slamming downstairs made both girls jump. Emma glared at Lana before they both hopped out of bed and ran to their bedroom door which they opened, looking down over the bannister.

'Dad?'

Peering up at them from the bottom of the stairs stood an attractive grey-haired man in his early 50s, taking off his soaking coat.

'Shhh, we don't want to wake Greg and Lucy,' he said as he summoned them downstairs.

'Oh Patrick, they should be in bed too,' whispered a voice from the kitchen as the two girls skipped down to find out what was going on.

'You know what they're like, Audrey,' he said as he hung his dripping coat on the stand in the hallway. Tutting, his wife promptly removed it and placed it in the sink in the downstairs cloakroom before going back to kiss him.

'What's happened, Dad?' asked Emma as she sat huddled up to her sister on the bottom step. A clap of thunder made her jump and she shivered, her eyes wide open with apprehension. Lana rolled her eyes and put her arm protectively around her sister.

'Let's have a cup of cocoa,' Audrey said, recognising the look on her husband's face. There was bad news.

While they waited for the milk to heat up on the stove, Lana went into the lounge looking for candles as the lights continued to flicker, constantly threatening to go out for good.

'I've found some,' she said, setting them down on the kitchen table with a box of matches, 'just in case,' she smiled. 'So what's going on, Dad? Why did you have to go out so late?'

'He's the Chief Constable... it's his job,' answered their mother as she poured steaming milk into the four mugs, before stirring them as quietly as she could.

Lana stood beside her, adding a spoonful of sugar to her mug before passing the calming drinks to her family, who stood sipping the chocolatey goodness silently for a moment.

Rubbing his forehead, Patrick put his cocoa down on the table just as the rain began to clatter loudly on the roof tiles.

'Oh no,' whispered Emma as she pulled her feet up towards her bottom and rocked back and forth in her seat.

Patrick put his hand on her shoulder, 'It's okay sweetheart. It's just a storm, it'll pass. Everything will be all right.'

'Well then why did you have to go out in it, Dad?' she asked.

'I was called out to the old Grimshaw farm... Josiah was seen wandering close to the pier again.'

'What? In this weather? Does he have a death wish?' said Lana without thinking as her mother tutted, glancing towards Emma. 'Did you find him? Is he okay?'

'I'm afraid he's nowhere to be seen. And in these conditions, it's impossible to send out a search party. We can't send out the lifeboat without risking the lives of everyone else, I'm afraid. He's a silly old man, he should never have been left alone in this storm. Everyone on the island knows how it affects him.'

Audrey patted her husband's hand, 'there'd be no stopping him, love. He's just looking for her.'

'Well, maybe he's finally got his wish.'

'Daddy?' said an innocent child's voice from the stairs.

'Oh we've woken the kids,' said Audrey as she stood up and went to check on her two younger children.

'Hey, sweetheart. Sorry we woke you. Come on, let's go back to bed,' she said to her family. 'There's nothing we can do now. We should all try and get some sleep.'

oOo

'You awake, Sis?' asked Lana later that night.

'Of course I am. There's no way I can sleep in this,' said Emma as she snuggled deep into her quilt.

'It'll be over soon.'

'I hope so, it's been going on for hours. I just hope old Mr Grimshaw is okay.'

'Yeah, I know. Do you know why he was out?'

'No, I haven't got a clue who he's looking for. I was going to ask Mum before Lucy came down.'

'We'll find out tomorrow. Try and sleep Em,' Lana said as she rolled over and closed her eyes.

Emma let out a deep sigh and pulled the cover back over her head. "Night Lana.'

The next morning Emma sighed as she peered over the edge of the cliffs towards the view below, wondering if Mr Grimshaw had been found yet.

The beach was scattered with pieces of driftwood, big and small, and masses of seaweed covered the expanse of sand and pebbles. The calmness of it all belied the furious storm that had battered the island the night before.

Squinting, a breath halted in her throat as she spotted something unusual among the debris. 'Oh my God,' she whispered as she turned back up the garden path to the house and ran as fast as she could, shouting, 'Dad! Dad!...'

Patrick appeared from the back door, putting on his coat, his eyebrows knitted together, 'What is it? What, love?' he asked as she bounded towards him.

'There's someone... someone on the beach. It looks like a body, Dad.'

'Stay here love,' he asserted as he ran towards the cliff edge to take a look.

Sure enough, there was a body strewn on the sand below. It wasn't moving.

'Is it Mr Grimshaw, Dad?' she cried from beside him.

'Emma, you mustn't see this. Go back indoors, tell your mother what's going on and then stay put.'

Pulling out a mobile phone from his inside pocket, Patrick called for an ambulance as he began the climb down the steep path that led directly to the beach. Emma, who had quickly run inside and told her mother what was going on, soon appeared, following closely behind.

'Emma!' he said, 'go home.'

But his daughter confidently shook her head, 'I'm not a child any more, Dad, I'm fifteen and I'm coming. You might need help.'

Shaking his head, he said, 'At least stay behind me. You shouldn't have to see this.'

She nodded as they reached the bottom of the cliff and ran towards the body.

As Patrick checked for signs of life, Emma couldn't resist

peering at the pale young man whose dark brown hair was plastered across his forehead and closed eyes. He wore a dark blue velvet trimmed suit jacket, a shirt that was once perhaps white and loose-fitting black trousers with black leather brogues, all of which were soaked through and ripped in places. Little pieces of drying seaweed were dotted all over him.

'Is he... is he... dead, Dad?'

'He has a pulse,' said Patrick, 'it's weak though. Come quickly Audrey, he's still breathing!' he yelled as he spotted his wife climbing down the pathway with her medical kit.

'I've spoken to the ambulance and they're almost here...' she said, out of breath, 'mind out the way, love and let me have a look at him. Do you know who he is?' she asked as Patrick and Emma stepped back to let her do her job.

'Never seen him before. Do you recognise him, Emma?' he asked as she shook her head.

'Patrick, the ambulance is arriving over at the far end of the beach. They might need a hand getting the vehicle a little closer. Can you go and give them a hand? We're okay here, love. Emma can help me.'

Emma's eyes widened as she looked at her mother and she gulped.

'Help me with this love,' she said while Patrick ran to the other end of the beach. 'Emma, I need your help with this,' she repeated.

Crouching down, Emma did as she was told and held the boy's head in place while Audrey inspected him for injuries.

'Well I can't see any visible wounds to the body but that's not to say he doesn't have any internal injuries. We need to keep his head and spine perfectly still until they bring the stretcher. His breathing is very slow. What happened to this poor boy?' she said more to herself than to Emma. 'It's okay now, love, you can let go. I've got him.'

Emma released the boy's head and swallowed hard as she returned her arms to her side, but just as she did so, he suddenly moved and grabbed hold of her.

Gasping, Emma jumped and froze.

'Mum,' she cried as the boy's eyes opened wide and he looked right at her.

'Shhh,' said Audrey, 'it's all right, dear. You're safe now. Please stay still. Can you tell me your name?' she asked softly.

The boy said nothing, he just continued to stare at Emma who began to fidget nervously.

'Em, calm down, please. You must be calm for our patient.'

The boy's grip on her arm strengthened and she looked down at it, wondering what to do.

The arrival of the ambulance crew solved her problem, as they swiftly and carefully attended to him, placing him on the stretcher and carrying him back towards the ambulance. As he was placed into the vehicle, the boy suddenly groaned, before he yelled out, 'Em!'

Audrey looked at her daughter, 'I thought you didn't know him?' she asked.

'I don't, I've never seen him before. I don't know him, Mum, honestly I don't.'

'Em!' he yelled again, struggling against the equipment that was keeping him in place.

'Emma, you're going to have to come along for the ride. If having you here is the only way to calm him down, then so be it,' said Jeff, one of the Medics.

Audrey nodded and ushered her inside before she went to close the doors behind them.

'But Mum?' she said.

'There's no buts. We need to get this boy to the hospital as soon as possible, you're going with him.'

'Tell Lana where I am, please. Tell her to come.'

Audrey nodded to her daughter, finally closed the door and the ambulance began to drive away, with the boy gripping on to Emma's hand.

🙚 21 🙚

THE GHOST OF JOSIAH
GRIMSHAW 2

'I can't believe you left me at home,' said Lana, pouting outside the hospital after she'd cycled all the way there.

'You wouldn't have come anyway. I followed Dad to the beach down the cliff pathway. You know, the cliff that you're terrified of. You'd never have come down there. Besides, I had no choice... he wouldn't let me leave. It was... weird.'

'Yeah, I guess so. Do they know who he is yet?'

Emma shook her head and ran her fingers through her long brown hair. 'He's sleeping now. Are you gonna come up and see him?'

Lana grinned, 'Of course! You know how I love a mystery,' she said practically dragging her towards the entrance to the island's only hospital.

Emma smiled at her sister and shook her head as she was practically pulled through the electric door. They walked straight up to their father.

'Dad,' said Lana, 'Any news?'

Shaking his head, Patrick placed a protective hand on both his girl's shoulders. 'Afraid not girls. We don't know who the boy is, and there's still no sign of old Josiah. It's not looking good. The coastguard has been scouring around the island all morning.'

'That's so sad?'

'Dad?' asked Emma.

'Yes sweetheart, what is it?'

'Who was Mr Grimshaw looking for?'

Patrick was just about to answer when the walkie talkie he carried in his belt during working hours went off.

'Do you copy, Chief?'

Turning slightly away from his girls, Patrick held the gadget to his face, 'Ten-four, Duncan. What's going on?'

'It's Josiah Grimshaw, the Coast Guard pulled his body out of the water about a mile off the coast. He's alive but it's touch and go at the moment. Over and out.'

'Well I never... erm, Roger that, Duncan. I'm at the hospital, I'll await his arrival. Over and out.'

Placing the walkie talkie back onto his belt, he turned and smiled at the girls, 'this just might be a good day, after all. Why don't you girls go on up to our mystery boy? If he wakes up with you there, it might help to calm him. I'll be up again in a bit after I've checked on Josiah.'

Nodding, Lana and Emma gave him a quick hug before heading to the stairs where they ran up to the second floor and tiptoed into the boy's room.

'Oh... I was expecting a kid,' whispered Lana. 'He's not much older than us. He's cute.'

'Lana... for goodness sake,' said Emma as she tried not to laugh, 'but I guess so,' she added with a half-smile.

oOo

Half an hour later, a faint groan escaped his lips, making the girls jump.

'Em?'

'He wants you, Em. He just groaned your name,' said Lana with a smirk as she tiptoed to his bed and looked down at the handsome young stranger.

'Grow up, Lana,' she said as she shook her head.

'Em... is that you?' he muttered with his eyes closed.

'Well, come and speak to him then,' Lana demanded.

Reluctantly, Emma stood and walked slowly to his bedside, pushing Lana to one side.

'Erm, it's me. It's Emma,' she whispered.

He held out his hand towards her. Emma's eyes opened wide

and she turned to look at her sister who pushed her forward. 'Go on then.'

Inching her hand forward, she gently placed it in his. He squeezed it and opened his eyes. When he saw her he smiled, 'Em, is that you? I knew you'd come back to me.'

'But... but how do you know who I am?' she asked and he smiled.

'I could never forget you. I've been looking for you for so long.'

'You have?' Emma felt her cheeks burn while Lana sniggered behind them.

'Who are you?' she asked. He looked hurt.

'You don't know who I am?'

Emma slowly shook her head and he coughed.

'Please, may I have some water?' he asked with a hoarse voice.

Lana stepped out from behind Emma and filled the small glass from the pitcher that stood on a tray at the end of the bed. She handed it to Emma, who carefully placed the straw to the young man's lips.

'Thank you. Are you sure you don't know who I am?'

Again, she shook her head, 'I'm sorry but I've never seen you before.'

'That's impossible. You're my Em,' he whispered sadly. 'I finally found you after all these years and you don't even know who I am,' he coughed again, wincing in pain.

'Are you in pain?' asked Lana. 'Shall I fetch a nurse?' she said heading for the door.

'I... I... Em?' he wheezed as a coughing fit hit him full force.

'I'm sorry, I don't know what to do,' she panicked, bringing the straw in the glass of water to his lips again but his body began convulsing and so she stepped backwards in shock.

The door opened and a doctor in a white coat, followed by quite a butch nurse rushed in.

'Please wait outside girls,' she commanded.

Lana and Emma did as they were told, watching just before the door closed in their faces.

'What the heck was all that about?' asked Lana.

Emma looked at her sister and burst into tears.

'Em? I'm sure he'll be ok, Sis. Don't worry... he'll be fine,' she said, not quite as reassuringly as she'd hoped.

Pulling her sister away from the room, the two girls found a small sofa just down the corridor opposite a large window that looked across to Carlton Point, the highest point on the island.

Patting the seat next to her, Lana smiled as Emma sat down and leaned her head on her sister's shoulder.

'I wonder why he thinks he knows you. I wish we could find out who he is,' she sighed just as Patrick appeared at the top of the stairs at the far end of the corridor. Before he noticed them, he walked into the boy's room, only to walk out moments later holding his hat close to his chest with his head lowered.

Spotting them, he smiled sadly and walked quickly towards them.

'Dad?' asked Emma.

But their father just shook his head, 'He's fallen into a coma. It's not looking good, I'm afraid.'

Emma's bottom lip quivered. Noticing, Lana took her hand in hers and squeezed.

'And Mr Grimshaw?' Lana asked.

'He keeps drifting in and out of consciousness,' he replied, shaking his head sadly, 'it's the same situation as the boy. Touch and go. I must get back to work. Are you girls going to head home?'

Emma shook her head, 'I want to stay here a while longer. I'd like to stay with him, if that's okay, Dad?'

'Course it is, sweetheart. I'm sure he'd like that. I'll see you at dinner,' he said, kissing each of them on their cheeks before placing his hat back on his head. He walked back down the corridor towards the stairs.

'I can't stay, Em. We arranged to meet Scott this morning, remember?'

'You go. I think I'd rather be on my own here anyway.'

'You sure?'

Emma nodded, 'I'll walk home later on.'

Lana said goodbye and wandered down the hallway, turning to watch her sister calmly walk back into the strange boy's room alone.

THE GHOST OF JOSIAH
GRIMSHAW ₃

Outside, the harsh sunlight made it hard to believe that such a ferocious storm had unleashed itself on the island the night before. Apart from the debris piled across the beach, the only other proof of the event lay fighting for their lives in two different hospital rooms.

Lana removed her leopard print cardigan and shoved it into the handbag she wore across her chest before shovelling around to find her favourite over-sized black sunglasses. Putting them on, she flung her bag across her back and climbed onto her bike, pushing away from the hospital and onto the main road.

Scott had been waiting for 25 minutes and was just about to leave when he saw a lone figure cycling uphill towards the castle ruins where they so often met.

'Hey!' he shouted, 'You're late!'

Lana stuck out her tongue childishly and grinned at her and Emma's best friend who stood, waiting impatiently. As she pushed the pedals the last few metres, the blonde-haired boy removed the small rucksack from his back, again, and dropped it to the floor.

'Sorry,' she huffed, 'you'll never believe what happened,' she gushed.

'Where's Em?' he asked.

'Give me a minute, I'm getting to that...' she said as she

climbed off the bike and let it drop against the crumbling walls of the ancient castle.

'This unconscious guy was found on the beach this morning. Dad and Emma were the first ones down there to help him and when he opened his eyes, he recognised Em. He won't let her leave his side. It's seriously weird.'

'Who is he?' asked Scott as they walked through their favourite archway and sat on the fallen stones where they'd sat a thousand times before.

'Nobody knows, but he sure seems to know Em.'

'So where is she?'

'He fell into a coma at the hospital and she doesn't want to leave him.'

Scott smiled, 'She's such a softie, your sister.'

Lana pretended to be offended, 'And I'm not, you mean?'

'I think you know the answer to that,' he replied, as he shoved her shoulder playfully.

'Well, I guess I'm not quite as soft-hearted as she is, I suppose.'

'You reckon?' he laughed.

Lana rolled her eyes and looked through the archway towards the rolling green hills and numerous wind turbines beyond, 'Did you hear about old Mr Grimshaw?'

Scott nodded, 'Did they find him yet?'

'Yeah. He's in the same condition as the young guy. Weird, huh?'

'I guess. Let's hope they both make it.'

Lana nodded and stood up, 'Do you wanna go for a ride?'

'Sure,' he said as they wandered back to their bikes. 'Where do you want to go?'

Lana shrugged her shoulders.

'We could try and get up to Carlton Point?' Scott said with a straight face.

'You are joking, right?'

A chuckle escaped his lips and he nodded, 'Yeah, I know, I know. I wouldn't put you through that. Don't worry, we'll stay on low ground.'

Before he knew what hit him, Lana gave him a swipe with her handbag, nearly knocking him to the ground.

'Haha, very funny Scottie.'

'Don't call me that,' he laughed before hopping on his bike, 'Come on, I'll race you!'

'Hey, so not fair,' she laughed as she raced along behind him.

But just as she reached him, she heard him curse as his mobile began ringing.

'That'll be Mum, she said she'd call me if she needed my help today,' he said, slowing down.

'Aww but it's a Saturday, Scott.'

Raising his eyebrows, he pulled the phone out of his pocket, 'Hey Mum... yeah okay. I'll be there in fifteen.'

Clapping the phone shut, he turned to Lana, 'Jeanie had a bit of an accident and had to pop down to the hospital so Mum needs my help in the shop.'

Lana's angry expression vanished, 'Oh, is she okay?'

'And there I was thinking you weren't a softie,' he laughed, adding, 'yeah, she'll be fine. She just cut herself on broken glass. It's a nasty cut and needs a few stitches. I'd better go though. Maybe see you later?'

Lana nodded and shooed him away. 'Go,' she said with a smile, 'I'll see you later.'

Staying put on the side of the road, Lana watched him cycle away into the distance. She didn't want to go home and she certainly didn't fancy going back to the hospital, so she hopped back onto her bike and took an easy ride towards the old church-yard. As she approached the crumbling remains of the building that had been destroyed in 1953, she kept a close eye on Carlton Point which stared back down as if goading her.

But instead of pulling up at the churchyard, something made her continue cycling. It was if they weren't her legs pedalling. She just kept going. Breathless, her heart thumped in her chest as she came to a slow about halfway up the steep hill. Stopping, she climbed off and pushed her bike to the grassy expanse to the side of the pathway, letting it fall to the ground. She followed it and sat down for a few minutes, getting her breath back.

The wind picked up temporarily and with it came a gentle sound. It sounded like someone calling out her name. Turning to look up towards the very top of Carlton Point, Lana couldn't see anyone. It's just my imagination, she thought. It's just because my heart is beating like God knows what. But the sound continued persistently: 'Laaaanaa..... Laaaanaa... Laaaanaa...'

'What the...?'.

Standing, Lana did a full circle squinting her eyes before chuckling nervously, 'Very funny, Scottie. I know it's you. You can come out now!' she yelled.

But nobody appeared.

She fidgeted with her fingers nervously. She planned to climb back on her bike and cycle away but her legs moved in another direction: towards the summit.

No, she thought, no...

But it was no good. She no longer had any control over her body and she continued walking until she reached the pinnacle of Carlton Point. Lana was terrified. She'd always had what she thought to be an irrational fear of heights. Just like Emma had an irrational fear of water. There was no explanation to either phobia. Then why am I here? Why did I climb up?

At the very top of Carlton Point was a small circular patch of ground surrounded by an ancient stone wall. On one side of it was the pathway she'd just walked along... although steep, there were no scary edges as such. But the other side was an altogether different story. She'd seen it in pictures, and from afar, but she'd never seen it up close.

Standing dead centre as she let her handbag fall to the ground, Lana closed her eyes just for a second. I'm not here, she thought, I'm in bed having a nightmare. But the gentle breeze told her a different story. She gulped hard and opened her eyes, her limbs incapable of moving further. But she was no longer in the centre of the circle. She was now looking down at a sheer drop hundreds of feet below.

She could hear her heart beating, feel it thudding in her chest. She couldn't open her mouth; it was too dry. All she wanted to do was scream but she couldn't even do that. Please, God, don't let me die, she thought.

A sudden massive gust of wind took her feet from beneath her and she was forcefully pushed from the top of Carlton Point, falling silently and peacefully to the rocky hills below.

oOo
The Ghost of Josiah Grimshaw is available from most online book retailers

ABOUT THE AUTHOR

Suzy Turner wrote her first chick lit novel in her early twenties, but it wasn't until much later that she decided to focus on writing full time. It was during a visit to Canada in 2009 when the ravens within the dark eerie forests of British Columbia called to her. The story of Lilly Taylor was born soon after and the first novel in The Raven Witch Saga was created. Suzy has since published several more urban fantasy books (under her pen name SG Turner) and contemporary women's novels.

Having lived in Portugal since childhood, Suzy, who is originally from Yorkshire in England, loves to travel. She finds inspiration wherever she goes. Old decrepit buildings, graveyards, cathedrals and castles are just a few of the things that can be found within the worlds of her urban fantasy books, and her contemporary women's fiction novels are filled with fun friendships, ordinary people in extraordinary circumstances and quirky characters you'd want as friends.

Suzy lives in the Algarve with her husband, three cats and a dog, where she does yoga every morning and bookish stuff for pretty much the rest of the day!

For more books and updates, visit www.suzyturner.com or www.chilloutpress.com

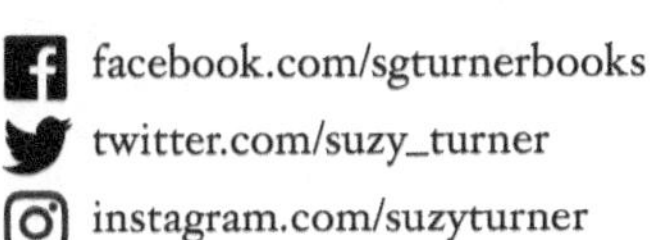